#BelieveAmerica

How I tried to end mass shootings and accidentally started a cult

GUERNICA WORLD EDITIONS 65

#BelieveAmerica

How I Tried to End Mass Shootings and Accidentally Started a Cult

Samson Johnson

GUERNICA
World
EDITIONS

TORONTO—CHICAGO—BUFFALO—LANCASTER (U.K.)
2023

Guernica Editions Founder: Antonio D'Alfonso

Michael Mirolla, general editor
Scott Walker, editor
Cover design: Allen Jomoc Jr.
Interior design: Jill Ronsley, suneditwrite.com

Guernica Editions Inc.
287 Templemead Drive, Hamilton (ON), Canada L8W 2W4
2250 Military Road, Tonawanda, N.Y. 14150-6000 U.S.A.
www.guernicaeditions.com

Distributors:
Independent Publishers Group (IPG)
600 North Pulaski Road, Chicago IL 60624
University of Toronto Press Distribution (UTP)
5201 Dufferin Street, Toronto (ON), Canada M3H 5T8

First edition.
Printed in Canada.

Legal Deposit—Third Quarter
Library of Congress Catalog Card Number: 2023935221
Library and Archives Canada Cataloguing in Publication
Title: Believe America : how I tried to end mass shootings and accidentally
started a cult / Samson Johnson.
Names: Johnson, Samson, author.
Series: Guernica world editions (Series) ; 65.
Description: First edition. | Series statement: Guernica world editions ; 65
Identifiers: Canadiana (print) 20230201857 | Canadiana (ebook)
20230202136 | ISBN 9781771838184 (softcover) | ISBN 9781771838191 (EPUB)
Classification: LCC PS3610.O377 B45 2023 | DDC 813/.6—dc23

*"The Americans are quite crazy.
They are always seeking;
we don't know what they are looking for."*

—Pueblo Chief Mountain Lake to Carl Jung

1

I CAN ONLY SAY THINGS HAVE been better than they are right now. Day in, day out though, the meds are easy to knock back, the staff are nice, and the furniture in the therapy rooms is fairly comfy. I never thought I'd end up in one of these places. I guess no one ever does.

A setting like this is kind of a peculiar non-space for a lot of the time you find yourself in it. Depending on how everyone on the ward is doing, we usually go down to the canteen for our three meals a day. Though this doesn't always happen, if there's enough "fires to put out" up here, the food gets brought up to us. The shrill blare of the staff alarm going off is a near sure sign that we will not be leaving the ward for our meals. That being said, the flood of wide-eyed staff bursting onto the ward and into the fray can liven up an otherwise uneventful day. On a handful of mornings, I've found myself hoping for a "quiet day" on our ward just for the chance to get anywhere else. Yeah, a two-hundred-yard, guarded walk to a canteen has increasingly become my idea of freedom. Hell, I even took up vaping just to give me a couple more opportunities in a day for fresh air. It's not been an exhilarating stay, but I've made some friends. Had my folks visit for the first time the other day, it went better than I expected. A lot of the people on our ward are hardly savants of conversation, yet in the passing instances I've shared with them, they seem nice. I definitely prefer the art groups to any of the therapy groups—people aren't thinking, aren't self-conscious in those things, you're more likely to actually talk to someone in one of the art groups. Not to mention, some people are just outright talented. There's this guy called Thomas, who as far as I'm concerned has "the gift." I can't really make out what people do or don't think of me on the ward; my therapist says that's something not to occupy myself with. I find it hard. From all our group therapy together, I've learned a lot about everyone on this ward, and I find my mind running over it a lot.

Everyone in here has had a "breakdown," but I've been realizing it's a very misleading term. When somebody tells you they "don't want to have a breakdown" or they'd "only go to therapy if they had a breakdown," they are thinking of a single moment. This is not the makings of a "breakdown." Any "breakdown" does not happen in a moment. In fact, most "breakdowns" are more akin to "burnouts" than most would like to consider: they happen over time, not in an instant.

I don't know when mine began, and I'm no longer in a position to claim when it's ended. Memory of that time is murky to me now, but man, I felt tired. I remember that much. It was like I'd already been awake a million hours. I was like a politics bicycle seat. I felt like I'd done every job under every stanchion of the entire political landscape. Plenty of janitorial work, and for the record, the janitorial in politics goes both ways: politicians and constituents are equally capable of being assholes. I've not enjoyed lying on behalf of either side of that binary. I'd also like to say, there's always dodgy money flying around, you've just gotta be high up enough to even see its movements. How the sausage gets made. Most of my experiences in the political field, however, haven't been that dramatic or thematic, more unfortunate, embarrassing.

I was campaign managing a while back for an Irupblecan candidate. I was paid handsomely, from a well-oiled machine; the guy owned half the properties in The Villages. He looked like something out of a '50s cartoon strip and spoke like one too. I didn't hear the fella curse once. "Yikes," "Jeepers," "Oh-boy-oh-gosh" and my personal favourite, "Consarn it!" Beyond the Howdy Doody-isms spilling out of his every pore, his puritanical approach to language was matched by a puritanical vision of family life. Every campaign stop, town hall and interview was punctuated by a wistful reminiscence of childhood. I'd speak to aides about how he might want to dial it down. How it was borderline creepy just how fondly he remembered all the "moms, permed and aproned" and all the "dads, hatted, lantern-jawed and briefcase-clutching." He was determined to finish every townhall meeting posing with his wife and children, picture perfect. As he'd take his wife's hand, he demanded he could be heard or lipread saying, "Still the best feeling in the world." This was his thing: "Family Values," and rigid gender roles all under the eyes of God—the clear repost to all of America's problems … according to his campaign.

I had the dreaded phone call about three months in.

"There's something I should have told you." A statement straight out of hell that could only mean bad news. It turned out my candidate had a very different life to the one his mouth had been going round telling the county. This opening statement queued details that were followed by "but there's more …" And boy was there. In fact, each admission was shortly followed by "more," till I felt I was listening to a podcast on Caligula. I was kind of staggered by the rampant escalation of it all. The tales started as instances of compulsive lust, but come the half hour mark, I was beginning to scratch my head as to how the stories even pertained to one's sexuality.

What started as tales of "bathroom stalls," "slinking off with X after a lingering gaze," "attending a seedy club at 3 am" had somehow grown into "strapped to a ceiling fan covered in lipstick and lighter fluid," "wearing a rubber dress surrounded by masked people lathered in goose fat" and "attaching one's nipples to a car battery while holding a fishing rod and singing Greek Orthodox hymns." Perhaps most hilariously, the candidate asked *me* what *they* should do about it. My lack of expertise in nipple abuse with car batteries had left me speechless. Staggered to the extent of my client's rampant hypocrisy, I figured I'd try the candidate's own spiel on him.

"Have you asked God? Have you spoken to Jesus?"

"HEY, I'M TRYIN' TO BE SERIOUS HERE, YA JACKASS! What the hell do I do? This could finish me. Integrity is important, honesty is important, I can't not run without either."

The triple double negative nearly left me with a nosebleed. However, the candidate was right, honesty is important, integrity is important. In the words often quoted by the candidate, "The truth shall set you free ..." So, my mouth ran away again, and I told his wife everything he'd told me. She didn't say a word. As speechless as I had been, the candidate wasn't so speechless. In fact, he expressed a lot, not with words, mind you. I woke up in hospital with a bandaged face and a brace round my neck. All's well that ends well: the walking Viagra overdose had to pay my medical coverage. I was grateful it didn't take much legal prodding, and more so that I didn't have to manage his soon-flatlined campaign after the press found out.

Despite my tire, I'd just about got myself in a position where work wasn't killing me, and I was enjoying it. I didn't have to speak to journalists about bullshit. I didn't have to lie incessantly about the blatant.

"How do you respond to reports of what the mayor said about the prevalence of mosques in the county?"

"What is important to note is that there are many elements ..."

"Is it true that the governor has previously stood against pro-choice policies?"

"Our time is one of the internet, and what the internet doesn't appreciate is all which came *before* the internet ..."

"What is your response to reports that delegates are moving away from supporting the senator after revelations about his personal life?"

"It's amazing the responsibility that a journalist holds when asking such a question, it is pertinent at such moments that we ..."

Unpack and deflect and unpack and deflect and unpack and deflect, but I always hated that stuff, even when I got good at it ... well, good enough.

I'd managed to get myself a good data and research job in DC. In back rooms, basements, invisible work, it was a job that contributed but didn't drain my entire being. My job requirements meant sitting, laptop and no human contact—I could do that. I did want the frontline thrills of campaign stuff, but the more I had that, the closer I got to looking like a sack of shit. The older I was getting, the lack of "home" I had from moving about so much was beginning to take a toll. I needed somewhere to plant myself, and the capital made sense. I could grease about and get all the gossip from sitting in the right places on the right nights, but I wouldn't have to be in the game. Being a no one, just a data guy, and I could live with that.

What I hadn't considered so much was my general lack of daylight from doing think tank data work in Washington, DC. There isn't a basement workplace in DC that isn't a weird "situation room" wannabe. No daylight, dull grey and a stuffy silence that implies all those present are important. I think it took a toll on me. Three months in, one colleague asked if I was, "going to any support groups in the area." I pretty much stood there lifelessly till I murmured "no," then he lifelessly murmured "OK" before walking away. My sleep wasn't amazing either. I did not look great, I looked like *Children of the Corn: The College Years*. I don't know what was up with me. I think I'd spent so much time in and around cameras and appearance-savvy environments that looking less than the furniture felt like a release. If I wasn't "manscaped" and dressed to impress, I didn't give a shit and felt free. Having seen photos of me at the time, extremely poor choice; I know I said I wanted to "grease about," but maybe not become an actual turret of walking grease.

I realized I had to break my habit and get more daylight and human contact. Most lunchtimes I'd escape to the Mall and people watch over a usually sad-looking sandwich. Compared to previous responsibilities this was fine. I knew I looked like a nobody and didn't suggest attractive or dateable, but that was fine too. People weren't what I needed; I'd been in jobs surrounded by people all my life. For the first time in a life dedicated to making the politics of America work better, I genuinely found myself running out of steam.

When I started out in my mid-late 20s, my mind told me that the longer I was in the game, the further my convictions would form and deepen. Yet, this is not what happened at all. Maybe it was the landscape of America or maybe it was me, hell maybe it was both, but the further I got into politics, the more I did, the less I felt conviction or inspiration. There were just legions of assholes everywhere, across the entire spectrum on every side of every divide—I mean, I knew I had *my* assholes, the assholes I rooted for, but they were nevertheless assholes. It was the American thing, pine for the top of the top and don't mind what may fall along the way. That was the bit I couldn't reconcile, I'd seen too much, I had to purposely "*stagflate*" myself. I didn't want to be in a rat race that everyone loathed the cancerous by-products of, yet desperately vied to be involved in.

The research job was all about schools. Looking up all available data and, if lucky, getting out some research for public schools in America. I figured if I was working for the environments and betterment of the young, I couldn't be all that bad. There was some fear and guilt in the decision; this arrived about a month beforehand. I had to sit down in arrivals at Logan Airport and ask myself what the shit I was doing with my life. I hadn't slept more than four hours a night over the last two months, and it struck me like a brick.

Nobody knows you.

Nobody knows what you do.

You have nobody to know you.

Nobody cares.

This is what a lifetime of "service" had got me. Don't get me wrong, working for some candidates left me witness to little miracles. I helped a lady one time out in Missouri, who got the local infrastructure bill for her district passed through the legislature, and guess what?

SHE GOT RE-ELECTED!

Promises kept, things working better and happy constituents, it was good to be a part of that stuff. It made me feel like the "swamp" of politics was the only real opposition. That maybe there was such a thing as the "right thing." So, I looked to schools and kids and used a brain that could do spreadsheets and data and other such thoroughly boring things.

People watching on the Mall hadn't got me much. Just a lot of people wealthier than me quietly wishing my non-existence as they passed. Figured I needed to double down my "re-integration into society" efforts. I decided I should not be afraid to finish my day in a bar with a hard-earned beer as opposed to scuttling back to my shoebox. From one shoebox to another shoebox, *the shoebox Amtrak.*

It was several weeks into my re-joining daylight and society programme, when I walked into a bar a little way into the outskirts of DC. My end of day treat after a hard day's work. It was a small place, like an old faux Irish bar kind of layout. Down some steps, low ceilings, not the most pleasant of smells and only at its best when packed to the gills. Walking in, the place felt a little quiet, all things considered. I'd spent many a year backing the lies of many people, so there's always a paranoid streak in me, terrified that I'm responsible for such a quiet. No one took notice of my entrance, the lights dangling above the worn wooden tables had an aged flicker to them and the world kept spinning. I saw a bar stool ahead of me, dark-green leather over a wooden frame that no doubt had been fallen off of many a time. The bar felt hurt; there was a couple at a booth who were more muttering than talking. They were leaning in as if speaking the illicit. The bartender had a pudginess to him, a middle-aged guy, and even he had a kind of zoned-out stare on. The whole place felt heavy, so I asked to all three attendees,

"Has everyone in here had a worse day than me?"

The bartender shrugged his round little frame. He turned his head and gave me a look. He then looked over to the couple talking, and they looked back at him. Heavy lidded, he took the molding buttoned TV remote in his pudgy hand and turned on the tiny screen above the manky bar shelves behind him. The news report flooded out of the screen in searing imagery and piercing sounds. My head was raised staring at the screen and within seconds my ears went deaf. I remember bringing the beer bottle to my mouth, feeling the liquid hit my tongue but not tasting anything. The heaviness of the room had arrived in me. I didn't want to talk to or look at anyone.

Another school shooting. Another pile of dead children. Another line of grieving families. Another aggrieved charge from an indignant left. Another claim of conspiracy, silence or indifference from a mangled right. Another school shooting. Another room full of hurt people nowhere near what happened. Another chance to rant, rave, declaim and express and another time when nothing changes.

Sitting on my bar stool, I soon realised I was physically shaking. I could not get comfortable and my hearing did not want to return to me. I don't know what happened next that night. I know that I got banned from ever going in that bar again. I woke up with a torturous headache and some real raw-looking hands. I know I did not feel the same from that morning onwards. I know that my hours in my data job increasingly became misused for gun research in America. I know that I couldn't sleep so well and my life seemed to get faster and faster. I think my "breakdown" began in that pokey little Irish bar on the outskirts of DC.

2

IT ALL STARTED WITH A giant mind map on my wall. I'm aware
that's not the best of signs. However, I was planning to *stop*
people from hurting people. "Guns" were the island in the
middle of the map. The first strand connected off "guns" was the
Second Amendment. That could not be moved, first obstacle. The
second strand connected off "guns" was the NRA. That could not be
moved, second obstacle. The third strand was "cultural normaliza-
tion." Again, this was decades and generations of lived experience;
this could not be moved. For every obstacle, I put a pink Post-it
note by the relevant topic on the wall. Twenty minutes into my
endeavor to protect America from itself, I had a giant Post-it-note
labia on my wall. I was charmed but intimidated and took a break
via an energy drink and hit my laptop to look outside the States.

When the UK and Australia took the move to end gun violence
thanks to mass shootings of children, it was truly a collective effort.
In fact, what made that work was that everyone handed in their
guns. The image of state for state, culture for culture, community for
community en masse handing in their firearms, that looked beyond
a cartoon to me. I put "national armistice" up on the wall and gave
it the relevant pink Post-it for "obstacle," as that was never going to
happen in America.

My fourth strand off guns was "trusted gun owners" ... which
turns out to be most of them. Everyone knows the dudes out in
spacious states with the scenery. But the hard reality is, most people

with a gun in America ain't going around capping people. And yeah, the rural folk who love hunting—they wanna pop an elk not a person. How's this ever been their problem? The fourth strand got another pink Post-it for "obstacle." I couldn't punish the minority who respected the gravity of taking a life with a gun.

I looked up at my wall and the giant "mind map" labia was staring right back at me. I felt like I was smashing my head through thick pine. Another idea arose: "militarization of police," so another pink Post-it went up on the wall. They love that shit, even if they can't afford a new squad car. Nothing is going to convince our police they don't need guns. Even if they now have notoriously too much and far too-overpowered weaponry. Ah well, I guess nothing says "law and order" like blasting a candy bar-stealing seven-year-old with an RPG.

I looked back to the stats. The predominant firearm of choice, and the one doing the most damage in American society, was the handgun, not the fully automatic, '80s Schwarzenegger movie guns. (Met him one time at an OGP do, he's alright.) It's the slip in glove compartment, under the pillow, into your belt or hidden in a purse handgun. I looked up at the giant mind map pussy on the wall and it had only grown in pomp and splendor, it was flowering. Another strand off guns, "W.O.C. = Handgun" and another pink Post-it. *Jesus Christ*, I thought, *this is why there's a giant vagina on my wall, this is what life's telling me: we're getting fucked.*

I was slumped on my couch. In truth, slumped on a pile of unwashed laundry on my couch. My mind started making leaps, and I went to the tooth and nail of the matter: if the institutes and culture can't budge, what about the people? How to change the minds of those with guns? How to maybe make the gun owners of America feel like they didn't want to own guns anymore. I had a spiral of ideas where I set up a click-bait stream of disinformation that would flood the IP addresses of NRA members with some prime bullshit. Figured if I could get gun owning tied to "socialism" or "communism" or "homosexual" or "mosque" then maybe hearts would turn. Then I reviewed the equation; efforts plus methods equals ethical quagmire and undermining democracy. My new-found plan was shortly dropped.

There wasn't much light coming in through my two windows of the shoebox. The oppressive grey of modern metropolis dwelling had filled my environment and I'd lost my step. What in God's name was I doing? How the hell was any of this supposed to be changed? How in good Christ were we tied to the slaughter of children "just because"? I don't know how long I was thinking this: it could have been minutes, it could have been days. The only interruption I had to this impasse and block was a dissociated daydream. It was like my mind was trying to tell me something, but it didn't seem all that relevant. I kept seeing a hand shaking another in slow motion, it kept playing in my mind's eye, on loop.

I soon recognized the hand from a memory. It was the hand of a mayoral candidate out in Acheron. I was doing polling for him. His hand was shaking that of a local imam; however, this imam was dead set *against* my candidate until they reached an "exchange." This candidate had recently gone to a townhall meeting of concerned parents over an "influx" of "foreign faces" but pulled off their favor by promising to instill Christianity back in local school prayer. This same candidate then assured the local imam that local enterprise would take "opportunities" of Middle Eastern Americans seriously. This was the way to get his photo op handshake and ensure the favor of this demographic. THAT WAS IT! Politics is exchange-based: find a way to get what you want by giving people what they want! Or at least say you can …

It was obvious what the powerful interests on the pro-guns side wanted: profit. The NRA and gun manufacturing was a machine with imagery attached to it, gun and ammunition sales was a behemoth of American capital that wouldn't ever want to change. I went back to the stats; I needed to think from the other side. I needed to read the stories of folks who'd survived shootings, any and every tale. This was the grimmest part and made me long for the chain-smoking days of my twenties. Sifting through the internet, most were riddled with psychological elements, the shock, the horror, and trauma, these the most common strands. Families of victims recurringly reported how their lives had changed since, only darkness; I saw no *profit*. There was another theme from all the reporting of shooting victims, the second most common strand, and it was telling: bills. As if someone holding your life in a single bracket of their finger wasn't humbling enough, when one is to survive such a horror, you then have to foot the bill for likely the worst ordeal of your life. I was hit by a surge of adrenaline, I'd found my ray of light … the insurance companies.

The most powerful lobby in our politics arguably, those with the power to dictate who lives or dies in America on the weight of their paycheck. They were the only possible profiteers from shootings. Sure, many people will die, lives will be lost, but between the bullet holes in the walls, windows shattered and those who survive, nothing breathes insurance like disaster. Everything in my apartment went quiet, the shoebox found stillness of near mystic proportions. I was struck by … the only conclusion:

> *Guns are killing people. But we can't get rid of guns.*
> *Outside of the loss of life, the collateral damage of shootings*
> *is profitable for the structurally important insurance companies*
> *of America. So …*
> *Guns are here to stay …*
> *But it's only the killing bit that … fucks everything up … so …*
> *Keep the guns and the shooting as it's "good for the whole" …*
> *Just get rid … of … the killings.*

I stared down at the mad scribble on my notepad telling me this conclusion. How long had I not slept? Why was I surrounded by a dumpster's fill of empty Red Bull cans? How did even my aftershave begin to smell like takeaway Chinese food? I was a mess. I stared down at the pad. I went for the nearest possible exploration of the idea, the mass production of non-lethal bullets. I knew conservative America would chuck me out of any town hall declaring me a "cuck" who needs to "find Jesus" before telling me "Americans know how to play with adult toys." (Honestly, I heard that doing press junkets out in South Carolina one time; not *a hint* of irony from the person saying this.) The non-lethal idea didn't sit right either. I knew non-lethals wouldn't pass as they'd further normalize the idea of people shooting each other. Moreover, the moment people accepted non-lethals there would still be bastards using lethals out there, making the whole enterprise a roulette not a guarantee of safety. *Son of a bitch ...*

I forgot to mention I hadn't been at work for a week. Well, what I think was a week. I can't fully confirm that. I don't think I'd slept that much either; I was focused on the project. I'd find myself waking up at various points of various days. Overcast, late night, sun shining, early morning, I didn't leave the shoebox. That being said, my acquaintance with the menu of the local Chinese place got intense. Whenever I think of sizzling beef in black bean sauce, a warm wholesome smile expands across my face to this day. I woke up one time and it was dark outside. I didn't check the time as there wasn't really a point to doing so. I went for a shower. I smelled. When you're sleep deprived enough, it's hard to tell where your stink is emanating from. I got that muddled logic where I was convinced the lack of sleep was making me smell. The shower was long.

As the water poured over me and I endlessly soaped myself like I'd been wading through the sewers, a single phrase echoed in my head: "Shootings are fine, killings aren't." I figured I'd shampoo my hair while I was in there. "Shootings are fine, killings aren't." Observing my feet, I realized I hadn't clipped my nails in a while and was beginning to look like the Gruffalo. "Shootings are fine, killings aren't." Nearly broke my stupid neck getting out of the shower to get the nail clippers. "Shootings are fine, killings aren't." Why on earth I thought clipping my nails would be easier in the shower, I don't know, but I went back under the water to clip them. "Shootings are fine, killings aren't." I finished my shower after like 40 minutes. "Shootings are fine, killings aren't."

I sat back down on the clothes-strewn couch, showered, looking like a prune but only borderline fresh. My giant mind map had been expanded and revised and had more colors to it than pink. *Your labia has evolved in to a … Labiachu!* My desk, never not the mess, was snowed under in printouts of polls and stats and studies all relevant to the gun landscape and shootings. Yet all of this aligned with all obstacles I'd laid out so far. There was also a glaring political culture that only supported what was echoing in my head; another binary, in a land of binary.

Guns are killing people, but you can't get rid of guns.

Cremodats say restrict gun ownership, Irupblecans say don't take away our guns.

Then I had … Shootings are fine, killing's aren't.

But wait … if I'm against killings but … I'm not taking the guns away, well god damn it, this is bipartisan. If this idea was pulled off right, both Cremodats and Irupblecans could actually get together on this. Yet, I knew this idea still predicated on the reality of shootings, so there was no guarantee people wouldn't shoot each other.

Unless …

What if people shot themselves? Not lethally, I don't want anyone to die, that's why I'm doing this. What if people shot themselves non-lethally? Like, it could be a communal kinda thing, like spiritual. Everyone gathers out in the woods; they make a circle and sit cross-legged, holding hands, and when the first verse of Kumbaya is done, everyone grabs a piece and blows a cap in their calf. That would feed the insurance companies and people wouldn't die. My god, who knows, if this got mandated at certain dates, hospital wards would be full of folks all there for the same reason. Hell, this could even build community relations as a *second order effect!!!*

I'd found it, my shining jewel of the insurance companies, they were the route out of this. The mandating at certain times made even more sense. If there was a yearly or bi-yearly, "yield of shooting," this could get structural significance and who knows, even institutional support. My mind then spiraled into how to sell this thing separately to Cremodats and Irupblecans. I needed a good pitch. The Cremodats would be easy if I avoided the specifics. Maybe, I could tell them that I was proposing a yearly or bi-yearly "gun tax" on all firearm owners. Maybe even propose this "tax" be dictated by the total accounting of costs in shootings for the given year.

#Gunshaveconsequences #makeamericasafeagain

The Irupblecans would be under my wing easily. This proposal made sure that not a single gun would be taken from not a single American exercising their right to bear arms. Furthermore, it would put responsibility and importance on the shoulders of American gun owners. I can remember thinking: If I could just play this right, if I could just get in the right angle of God and faith, well … the term "sacrifice" could come into play. The way God made a "sacrifice" of his only son for our sins. The way any proud American is willing to "sacrifice" to protect their rights and constitution.

#2ndAm4Evr #GUNSNFREEDOM

It was set up for me, the field was clear, I just needed to bust my ass to the yard line. This is America, I couldn't sit around waiting for things that would never happen, I had to get on my feet and make something happen.

So began my political movement to keep the guns without anyone getting killed. I realized, even in my addled mental state at the time, that this would take a great deal of faith. I knew in order to turn the tide, I would need people in on it. I would need numbers. This meant engaging in the one thing I had long imposed a self-ban upon. The global spiritual punch bag, the international opinion-off: social media. On the worldwide unacceptable feelings dump called "the internet," a Twitter account began under the name Save Lives, Save Guns PAC and my first post was humble and hopeful:

#BelieveAmerica

3

M Y MOM SAID I WENT into politics searching for my father. He had a different time and different gig from me. My father was a state senator for near 30 years. He was a trusted and loved figure back home. An older type of pol, the kind of guy who could reach across the aisle, knew how to pass votes, and make the necessary concessions without pissing off an entire district. Problem with Dad giving a lifetime of service was I never really met the guy. I used to say I caught his "entrances" and "exits." His "entrances" to the world from our front door and his "exits" from the world to our home, only to retire into an evening and night of phone calls. It's like politics swallowed him. He was never mean, never any form of abusive, but he always had his eyes on the prize and that was never his family.

Once Mark Johnson had retired from his 30 years of service, I guess my Mom thought she would kinda get her husband back, but that wasn't to be. He went into lobbying for every "moral cause" that had virtually no funding or backing. His silvery hair, loud blazers and moral vitriol decorated the local press as he continued his dedication. The older I got, the more prone he was to taking me around and showing me the channels of politics that he had carved out for himself. This meant meeting many "friends" and hearing the perspective on him from many. It was about 90 to 95 percent good. Then there were the occasional middle-aged ladies who would pop out of the woodwork with a loud tactile warmth for my father. My mom said I went into politics searching for my father. What mom didn't know was, I would never be on a search for a man who spent a lifetime balls deep in secretaries.

Work at the data job continued and I was grateful to be back after my apparent bar meltdown. Staff around the place began to show a special interest in me and my wellbeing. It was kinda nice. To be frank with you, since starting my data stuff in DC, I was more a headphones-in and nod kind of guy, and conversation was welcome. I found myself talking to our given data guru, Natalie. She was some 21-year-old brain on legs with a her hair permanently held back. She spoke like she was dictating minutes from a meeting, but she was super, super smart. In fact, frighteningly smart. I got the vibe she could obliterate any given soul in a three-line email.

For whatever reason, I ended up talking for a little bit with Natalie in passing. Which, at that point, only meant telling her that I wasn't really sleeping. Natalie delivered me a 10-minute mono-logue on the wonders of supplements and how since she started supplements she "hadn't even had to touch coffee." This sounded interesting, but where was the fun in life without coffee? Natalie wholeheartedly advised melatonin supplements; she said some-times when her head wouldn't turn off after long days of data and its entry, that stuff seemed to do the trick. She was kind enough to email me links to relevant sites and suppliers, and I sank a couple of hundred just on melatonin pills. I really missed sleep and I didn't want to take any chances.

Returning to my own data and analysis, I was studying through a pile of papers looking at the numbers of textbooks per classroom all across the country. The numbers were pretty unforgiving, and none of these reports held the environmental reality, what a lack of textbooks meant in a classroom already "overcrowded with chil-dren" or "understaffed with teachers." I could feel my feet tapping beneath me; I could feel myself wriggling in my chair and my body temperature rising of its own accord. My near full-body wriggling was soon interrupted with further methods of procrastination. Some idiot thought it was a good idea to give us all swivel chairs in the office. Some people travelled round this basement office space making their own sound effects to gliding across the floor. Ever the social scene enthusiast, I found myself rotating on the spot till I got lightheaded or nauseous. I ploughed along through the studies and stats despite my innards disagreeing with such a plan. It was soon to be lunch time, soon to have a break, and I wasn't committed to staying at work beyond lunch time.

I returned to the Mall with my signature sad sandwich. I did like being there, bang in the center of the capital. I'd heard from others working here about the special "tingle" you feel when you see the Capitol, how it was time to leave when that was gone. Back then, it was a tingle every time I sat on the Mall. I loved the vastness we all took for granted. The scale of America, the Washington monument, the war memorials, the richness of all of this and all the defiance that made it so. I'd find myself walking it a fair bit, you know. Sometimes, just sometimes, on the Mall, I did get the little thrill, that rush along the back of your neck, that swirl of excitement inside that tells you, you're proud to be an American. I looked down at my sad sandwich and I couldn't help but laugh, a real hearty chuckle. Fuck it, if Adam Smith lived with his mother, then I'm allowed a sad sandwich on the Mall sometimes.

The lunchbreak wasn't my motivation for getting to the Mall that day though. I hit the Mall for some privacy. It had been a couple of weeks since I started the Twitter account. I'd been posting a couple of things, trying out tag lines and re-tweetable stuff. Well, stuff that I hoped would be re-tweetable.

Protect the children, protect the Constitution, save lives, save guns.
#BelieveAmerica

We have a "gun problem." If the adults of America run from our problems, the children of America can never truly be safe.
#SaveLivesSaveGuns

When Congress is drawn to a halt, the people of America move,
for our rights, for our future, for our children.
#SLSG #BelieveAmerica

Action can overcome stagnation, truth can overcome falsehoods,
bravery can overcome tragedy.
#BelieveAmerica #SaveLivesSaveGuns

Nations have lost young to gun fire. Soul has been found, action
taken. We needn't be exceptional here.
#SLSG #BelieveAmerica

As our children cannot have their future stolen by a document
from the past, our Constitution cannot be soiled by the sinners
of today.
#BelieveAmerica #SLSG

Proud to be American, proud of the Constitution, proud of our
children, proud to protect them.
#BelieveAmerica #SLSG

It was a bit of a "Jesus Christ" moment when I logged back in after two weeks. The account had amassed 76,000 followers despite only 12 tweets and absolutely no specifics. I looked around the Mall to make sure no one was looking; it felt like I had discovered something haloed. Then my eyes met the inbox ... there were several thousand direct messages. People were genuinely interested in whatever the hell they thought this thing was. The majority all wanted to know where they could get in contact with the PAC. It had only been two weeks; I had not got near to starting up a PAC. I zoned out for a moment, realizing I'd have to start my own political action committee. I threw the sad sandwich away and got walking across the Mall. I didn't need to let work know I wasn't coming back.

The next spell of hours was some visceral blur of the senses. I began an impromptu field operation all on my own. My feet hammered asphalt till my legs were roaring with heavy blood, and I didn't care. I was organizing my next fifteen actions on my phone while walking. I was placing orders, checking directions, making phone calls, catching buses, sending emails all while making my way through DC. First stop was to get to a copy shop and print the hashtags onto flyers. (I did also consider bumper stickers, but that was more for those of prior planning sensibilities.) I burst in like a lunatic, and the guy in the printing place flinched so hard he nearly whimpered. I'd forgot how much I'd been walking; my entire face was wet with sweat. The guy running the joint was simply happy I didn't hurt him. I got a rucksack and filled it with hundreds of flyers and began a spree of propagandizing that felt incredible. Sure, after four hours I began to tire physically, but every lobbyist, congressman and politician that passed through DC over the next 12 hours would see:

#BelieveAmerica
SLSG-PAC

I had a purpose again, or what felt like a "real" purpose for the first time. I knew I was at least a day away from the melatonin arrival, so I worked my way into the night. Approaching sunset, the shoebox welcomed me with its usual glum dourness. I got a shower and microwaved some takeaway leftovers. A quick trip along a search bar, and I got hold of all the local locations of meetings and committees of local social interest and political groups. I had more flyering to do. I looked around the shoebox and I got the strangest idea: "Maybe I should actually clean this place." I did. I got a new apartment without having to rent one, and I did it in about half an hour. The shoebox suddenly looked like a cozy, secluded nest in DC. As my keys left the apartment door and I rattled down my building's stairs, I felt completely at ease. Maybe sleep deprivation gets you *high*.

The first committee meeting I found was a little towards the outskirts of DC. It was a conference room as opposed to a town hall, and it looked kinda low in expression but felt full of feeling. Rows of folded arms and pursed lips met one young Black lady hosting the meeting. The air was kinda stilted from the back, and most of the lines of suits and pant suits seemed ready to blow. The host must have been early-mid-twenties, and she was halfway through her sentence when ...

"THE SCHOOL WON'T ACCEPT MY CHILD WANTS TO IDENTIFY AS A POSTBOX!!!!"

"*WHAT ABOUT THE MOBILITY ISSUES OF THE POLYPANGENDER SEA TROUT????*"

"DOES THE COMMUNITY MOSQUE KNOW IT WAS *ME* THAT DONATED TO THEM? IT'S IMPORTANT TO *ME* THAT THEY KNOW THAT *I* DID THAT!!"

"MY AMAZON ALEXA KEEPS COMING ON TO ME WHEN I'M GETTING OUT OF THE SHOWER! AI HARRASMENT NEEDS TO BE ON THE AGENDA HERE!"

Wailing indignance in the veil of morality, all while cutting off the Black person in the room from talking: I'd found ... *the liberals.*

4

THE ROOM TURNED INTO A low rumble of cross talking with occasional outbursts that got smatters of applause. This was the way such meetings usually went, without fail. All attendees take the "pleasure principle" of noise and attention and end up forgetting why they're in the fucking room. The arguing and confrontational element of grounds up social political stuff had never really fazed me. Maybe it was that I grew up in a quiet household; I just found the screaming and declaiming somewhat bewildering. Then again, school was a different picture full of pointless noise.

As a disclaimer, this is not a story I tell or have told to many. I am telling you this because it's the honest thing to do. In truth, it's something I've spent most of my existence avoiding. My name is Samson Johnson. I tend to go by Sam; it's easiest. However, Samson is not my full name. My mom was a delicate kind of soul who had an appreciation of the small things. Mom got her appreciation of the small things 'cus her Dad, Grandpa, was one of the millions of "Willy Lomans." Door to door sales, braces, shoes shined and pitch ready, that was how Grandpa paid for a house.

Mom would watch him go through everything he owned out of wear and tear. She always watched him come home with progressively world-worn stuff. She witnessed the cardboard in the bottom of the shoes for the holes. Moth-eaten jackets needed clever sowing jobs from Grandma to survive. Then, the story is, Mom had saved up enough of her own money one time to get Grandpa a brand-new briefcase, for a guy too modest to get new things. This was back in the '70s, around his retirement, and apparently this gift was quite the moment for them. Jump ahead a few years, my Mom and Dad conceived, and she wanted to pay tribute to her father in the naming of her first born.

My Mom in her nostalgia-laden madness had not envisaged what naming a child "Samsonite" would lead to. It's a bit of a trip having a "funny name" when you're barely at an age to register what a "funny name" is. I picked up letting the school registrar know to shorten my name to "Samson" by the third grade. I showed up 15 minutes early every single day of elementary school to make sure I could. If Mom ever ran late in the mornings, I turned into the kid from *The Omen*. High school was a little more to the point. The school registrar was less interested in the opinion of a greasy horror as opposed to a scared little boy. Within one week, the legend of "suitcase dick" was born. There were at least two years where anyone in class lacking stationery would ask if I could ... "*have a look in my dick*" for them.

In the conference room full of liberals, there was barely any order. The Black girl at the front listened to everything and did her most to guide it. She was positioned against a wall of wild belligerence. Leaning up against the back wall, I remembered I was there to flyer and spread the word. Arms were flying around, and voices were popping across the room. I should have just dropped the flyers on the table in the foyer. Then my mouth ran away again. I found myself dead center of the room, and everyone was looking at me, silent.

"I can't say I know how to solve the problems that everyone is bringing here tonight. It's certainly not why I'm here and it appears we're all struggling to get our bit of participation to count. First of all, god bless you all and thank you for having the strength and courage to be here and put what's important out in the airwaves. It might not feel like it here and now, but this is only making our politics stronger."

I had 'em, I really had 'em. Nobody stood—

"WHAT DO YOU WANT?!"

Ech.

"What do I want? I want the impossible and I've found the path to make that a reality, but I can't do it on my own with the people I've got; we need the public."

"What the hell are you talking about?"

"Take these for yourselves," I said with some authority. I started to pass round the flyers.

"I've spent a life in politics. I've spent a life in politics like my father before me. I never saw any point in life revolving around me; I knew I'd never be worth shit anyway. Yet I knew if I could make the world around me a better place, or at least better the elements that run the world, then I might have done a half-good thing. I have been with liberal candidates and conservative candidates. I've fought liberal causes and conservative causes—Folks, I'm too weak and checkered to have goddamn bias. I came here to talk to you straight. I got the contacts, I got the will, I just need the people and a bit of fire and I wanna go on a journey with you. I wanna go on a journey like no other. One where we don't argue on how things should be but agree on how they're gonna be. Where we don't have to sit in town halls or conference rooms or basements and yell but can come together and make a stand in agreement. Where the word 'we' isn't met with suspicion. Where having commonality isn't a surprise and, who would have guessed, it feels right. Where having found the tools to become a collective, we've made America a better place.

"I have a bi-partisan policy proposal that is viable to both sides of the aisle, and it's gonna bring a new dawn in America. Ladies and gentlemen, I have one request, that you *believe America*. The Save Lives, Save Guns PAC is the first step of policy motion to make sure we don't see one more goddamn first grader shot dead in school … where they should be protected from the world around them, not laid to waste by its weaknesses. So … who's with me?"

Silence. The majority sat looking down at their flyers. The millennials present had already retreated into their phones. The silence continued for a beat before a guy in a navy-blue suit and a very sparkling watch next to me piped up.

"All sounds good but how you going to get the Old Grandad Party to go along with this really?"

"You're assuming we haven't already. It is: save lives, save *guns*. We are not proposing that a single gun leaves the hand of any American. In fact, I want the gun owners to take the lead on this one, that way they are not the villains, that way 'guns' can't be placed as the opposition. That way we might be doing a much better job of protecting our children's lives, instead of infighting, inaction and bullshit."

That last one got applause; I knew it was my cue to leave.

"Check it out folks, we're tweeting. Anytime over the coming weeks, I look forward to seeing the support of anyone who wants this to end; *believe America* ..."

Had I had a mic, I would have dropped it. Over the next few hours going into night, I used Ubers and powerwalks to zigzag my way all around the capital. I made about four more meetings, and some went well, and some did not. I could tell I was somewhat spent from my awe-inspiring outbursts and mainly resorted to fly-ering or leaving flyers for folks to pick up. My favorite meeting of the night was a pet owners committee, and it took place in a Sears Catalogue Home and in a neighborhood called 'Chevy Chase' no less. There was a little old lady who came to answer the tall, regal door when I rang the bell. When I walked in, there was a small conglomerate of little old ladies decorated with spectacles and their pets, all little pooches, the kind you can stuff in handbags.

One time out in Florida, I did some campaigning for animal rights over the SeaWorld stuff, you know, "Give Shamu a break." I have memories of standing outside SeaWorld and its training facil-ities and yelling and lobbing paint at people. What got contentious for me, was when folks wanted to show up and ruin a day for a kid trying to see Shamu. Some campaigners didn't mind making a family day into a disturbing experience in the name of the cause. I certainly got the logic, *if you aren't drawing a line everywhere, are you drawing one at all?* Yet, I soon lost my impetus. Turns out Shamu still got pissed and occasionally ate a trainer, and half these activists couldn't be bothered to pick up their dog's shit on a walk. I left animal rights campaigning.

The meeting with the old ducks was genuinely charming. They were so happy to have me join their weekly union. All the furniture and upholstery were decades old, and I was informed "Margaret" was the owner of that lovely and pristine home. I took a seat in a tall-backed, 100-year-old armchair in a circle of them. I soon got served some warming lemon and ginger tea. Unfortunately, in this ornate and cozy town house style setting, the old ducks were rather keen to hear about my pet owning experience. Life is an improv. I made up some story about "my" chocolate lab named "Gunner" who crossed paths with a stretched Hummer and that was quite the experience for him. #PrayforGunner. Apparently I was there that night on interest of "safety for animals," who would have guessed?

After an important 40 minutes got burned through by these hosting extraordinaires, I needed to make a break and flyer some more. I informed them I didn't have the time that given evening to stay the duration. They expressed their dismay I couldn't stay; I could only say I wished to return, and I genuinely did. From this, I managed to pivot and get the Save Lives, Save Guns thing into conversation. Margaret tilted her head and tipped her glasses up her nose with a single finger.

"Oh sweetie, we aren't here to start a revolution. We have each other and our gorgeous dogs and that's why we are here."

Goddamn it, she had a good point. However, I had made a good connection with this demographic, and they were superb listeners. Then my mouth ran away again, and I informed them of my political past and how this led me to "what I'd been hearing on the Hill." The old dears in their floral blouses leaned in closely as the lie commenced. I informed them of an alleged bill that the right was even scared to bring up to the Hill. How I'd heard the Cremodats were labelling it, the "AK Forty Pooches Act." There were rumblings that a policy proposal from some neo-conservatives involved the weaponizing of handbag dogs. They were working on the idea, that a dog loyal and small enough, with enough training over time, could in fact operate ... a Colt .22. My "exposé" sent the room into shivers; my newfound friends and dog enthusiasts were appalled. The flyers were distributed, I finished my tea, expressed my gratitude to Margaret and headed out to flyer more.

When the committees and meetings had ended come the earliest hours of the morning, I found myself sitting back out on the Mall. It was dark, still and kind of creepy, and I had a couple of security guys ask me my business. I moved on each time. It was cold in DC at night; I was wrapped up but shivering somewhat. I looked down the Mall all the way till I could see tiny lights of cars and buildings decorating the darkness. The starting of a Political Action Committee sounded momentous and serious. Doubt began to fill me like the severe chill of the night air. Wrapping my body as tight as I could, I searched the realities online about what starting a PAC meant. Within five minutes, it was clear: it was meaningless. All I needed was a bank account, proof I was American and an able party to be a treasurer.

Andros Langford was a half-Greek Canadian guy I met in college. He had shaggy dark hair and eyes like a car's headlights; he tended to fill the room. The guy had a very sharp mind that breezed through every academic assignment it was ever set. The person blessed with that mind unfortunately had the discipline of a meercat on bath salts. He knew just as much about politics and how the system worked as I did. The difference was I'd dedicated my life to working in politics for approaching 20 years. Whereas Andros played saxophone gigs and mastered getting half hand jobs outside nightclubs for the past 20 years. He was smart but completely innocuous. If Andros had his saxophone and opportunity for mischief in life, he was sated. I picked up the phone.

"Hey."

"Sam, long time no speak."

"Yeah out in DC now, I've been here last few months."

"DC is dry man, whatcha doing out there?"

"I'm starting a PAC and I need a treasurer. That's why I called."

"You leaving me in charge of the money?"

"I prefer to say 'treasurer' because that sounds better than what you just said."

"For real? A PAC for what?"

"It's called the Save Lives, Save Guns PAC."

"Ambitious."

"You in?"

"Yeah sure, watchful eye and all that?"

"That's the one, and keep me regularly updated."

"Sure, wanna catch a beer sometime?"

"I'll let you know next time I'm out in Cali …"

It was too late to sleep but too early to go to work, so I walked around a fair bit. Organizing thoughts and making note of all the drop-ins I'd done over the last few hours. After enough time had been burnt, I walked into an early open diner; I had a bagel and a black coffee while I started the PAC on my phone. Checking what relevant PACs were out there was not inspiring. The most effectual PAC relating to guns was the North Carolina Gun Rights PAC that had clocked up about 50Gs. As a counter point, there was also the Families Against Assault Rifles PAC that had raised $200,000. Also, on the liberal side there was "MUSICIANS AGAINST GUN VIOLENCE" which had clocked up about 0 dollars. Thinking about it, that might be another way to get people to shoot themselves: threaten a lecture from Bono. The coffee was curious, my hand shook so much the mug nearly didn't make my mouth. An email notification on my phone, told me a package probably containing my melatonin arrival had been "delivered safely."

5

BACK IN MY BASEMENT BUNKER of data and research, my latest glory was reports from the AFT (American Federation of Teachers) on public schools. You know if you are a teacher in America of 20 years-plus experience, you're probably to retire at the poverty level because we set up a myth that the "noble" have the constitution to be poor. If you're a new teacher in America, nobody's given you a heads up you're likely to spend about 1000 dollars a year in out-of-pocket expenses because the classrooms aren't stockpiled. You know if you're a teacher in America responsible for the state testing of, say, fifth graders, there's gonna be over 40 children to a classroom and about six broken laptops between them. If you're a teacher in America, your hope is that crowdfunding will save you. You know if you are a teacher in America who's concerned about children's expression, not only their ability to complete tests, you may find yourself a $100 arts budget allocated for 800 students.

I woke up at around 3:20 pm. I had crusty crap all in my eyes and the whole basement was in stitches. My colleagues decided in the event of me falling asleep sitting bolt upright I should not be woken from my slumber. Moreover, I should have a cock and balls marker penned on my face and my open salivating mouth should not be closed but used as a basketball hoop for tiny folded up pieces of paper. In their defense, a handful of people made the hoop with some amazing three pointers, I was told. On the other hand, I apparently ate these pieces of paper thrown into my mouth while asleep, all four of them. Although that did make sense of the scratch in my throat.

Once I had found my bearings and realized I was on planet earth, I went to the bathroom to wash off the face graffiti. Someone must have had a bank shot that didn't go so well; I found a piece of paper up my nose. Having made my attempt to freshen up, I walked back in and there was a silent contempt to the place: I returned to my desk as the guy who brought an end to the NBA office finals. Having been knocked out, I felt none the fresher, just groggy and disorientated. I logged onto my laptop and the screen came back to life. My eyes met a report that out in Oklahoma there were over 2000 untrained, emergency teachers. My innards began to sting, and my throat got all tight, my exhales got heavy and colorful. Natalie swiveled round in her chair and tilted her head at me. She then said in a lifeless, toneless voice, eyes wide, "Mel. A. Toe-nin." She had a point.

In a scuffled kind of hurry, I found myself packing up all my documents and laptop and heading out of the basement. A ferocious blast of wind struck me the moment I reached outside. DC could get so unforgivingly cold. My satchel was over my shoulder, and my pockets were filled with my clenched hands. It was still relatively light out, and the human traffic filling the sidewalks was low. My legs marched me closer to the innards of DC. I got out my phone and a fierce shiver ran through me as I ordered an Uber. Reagan National was my destination; I was getting a flight out to Oklahoma. If anyone asked, I'd put it under expenses for the think tank.

For barely over 200 bucks I got a ticket to Oklahoma City direct. Maybe out of a sense of sadism I picked United Airlines. In my defense I took necessary precautions. I checked if there was a rattlesnake in the overhead, or if there was a flight attendant looking like they'd slept less than I had. After some gratuitous rumbling and pre-turbulence on take-off, we were in the air, and I was but another poor soul cramped up in coach. To my relief there was not a horrifying reptile having a bad day in the seat next to me. Instead, there was a lady reading a glossy magazine. She looked mid-late 50s and was sitting upright, her hair was dyed loudly, and she kept her hard-shouldered beige overcoat on for the duration of the flight. Figured I try some polling.

"Excuse me. Can I ask you a question?"

Not moving her eyes from the magazine, her motionless mouth said, "What would that be?"

"I'm a pollster, er, well, a … er, I work in and around, I do a lot of policy stuff and—"

"I get it, what do you want?"

"One question. Is that OK?"

"Get to it," she said, still yet to look at me.

"What are your feelings on the Second Amendment?"

Her shoulders jumped up in a single chuckle. She slowly closed her magazine and tilted her head down to look at me. She blinked. She then looked around the cabin a little before leaning into me. She purposely kept her soft-toned whisper,

"Can I ask *you* a question? Maybe two?" I didn't respond because that wasn't an answer and I was quietly hoping she wouldn't hit me.

"Do you feel in present day America, we need to be defending ourselves from the British? Or do you feel in present day America, we need to ward off the Native American population?" She went back to reading her magazine and we sat in silence till we hit the tarmac in Oklahoma City.

Collecting my luggage was a breeze on the grounds I didn't have any. Found myself in a diner a little way along from the city center. I asked the cab driver if there was any place he would recommend, and there I soon was. It had one of those once shiny steel exteriors with the broken green neon sign up top. A place that couldn't let the 1950s be bygone. Walking inside, a couple of glances let me know my metropolitan attire wasn't making me fit in. While it wasn't busy, the diner was far from empty. The booths were sprinkled with families and folks all picking at baskets of food. There was a free stool up at the counter, so I placed myself upon it. I ordered a black coffee and a slice of Key lime.

The two stools to the left of me had occupants as well. To my immediate left, there was a huge fella whose lower half seemed to engulf his stool beyond visibility. It made it look like he had a thick metal pole running straight up his ass. He was wearing a tired-looking flannel shirt. From what I got in a glance, he had a somewhat pubic beard on a luxuriously full face. Next to him was a gaunt old boy. Pale as a milk bottle like his round counterpart, he had his spectacles in his shirt pocket and waist highs that appeared to be eating him. They were talking in a breezy, ponderous ease exploring the finer details of life. Then I started listening in over some quite fine Key lime.

"See … you go'n Walmart, you find them stockin' up chickpeas they call 'em."

"Whats a chickpea?"

"Some A-rab shit; we's accommodatin' them."

"What's an A-rab want a chickpea for?"

"That's how they makin' their hummus."

There was a beat of pause between them. The older gentleman mused: "Ain't the Greeks done hummus?"

"AW shit, yeah, maybe they did, prob'ly had a big ol' war over it sometime. They got beards too them Greeks but I don't think that's a Muslim country, but I don't know; maybe the A-rabs are Greek and the Greeks are A-rab, how we supposed to know?"

Further pause arrived.

"What's that tahini then, who done that?"

"Where's you hearin' 'bout tahini from?"

"I heard about tahini from the hummus."

"AW shit, that's prob'ly stuff that does your brain. That's prob'ly how they doin' it. The gosta get you doin' it five times a day remember. Maybe that's the hummus; 's all for the tahini. Few dollops o' that, 'fore you know it, you're leapin' up sayin' 'Alluh Akbar' involuntary. Just ruinin' shit; visit to your mom, kids' birthday parties, campin' trips … Goddamn hummus."

"You think I should be worried 'bout harissa?"

"Now, that ain't the A-rabs; that's the Latinos."

"The Latinos …"

"See, harissa is the 'chilli' in the 'con carne'."

"Now *THAT STUFF* just makes me shit!"

"Me too, gets me thinking that's what they want."

"Huh?"

"We all takin' too many bathroom breaks at work, then the Latinos look like better workers 'cus they ain't shittin' all the time."

"So, they employ more Latinos."

"That way they can undercut the wages."

"Shit…"

"See, I know what I'm talkin' 'bout."

"What they put in that anyway?"

"Hm?"

"Harissa, what's in that?"

"Prob'ly Mexican varmints."

"They got varmints out there???"

"Prob'ly."

The older gentleman paused again, before interjecting with caution: "I … I … I've had some *good* chilli."

"Yeah, I've had some good stuff too."

"My … my … my wife, she … er, she makes that hummus stuff and … I liked it when I tried it."

"Yeah, had in a wrap once with sum chicken, 'salright."

A pregnant pause arrived.

"Strange thinkin' all them interestin' flavors ain't from here."

"AW shit, all we's got is corn starch and diabetes …"

I'd finished my slice of pie and figured these philosopher kings might be able to help me out regarding local committees. Shuffling on my stool I made a lean over to the big moose.

"Say fellas, I couldn't help but overhear you. My name's Sam. Flew out here on behalf of a think tank lookin' at constitutional rights. You fellas reckon you'd be able to guide me in the direction of any local committees, office holders, that kinda thing?"

He shoved a finger in his ear, and gave a good scratch before informing me. "We's got a meetin this evenin' that's just 'bout down the road. It's about the county treasurer, don't know if that's useful to yus? You say you're looking at constitutional rights?"

"Well, yeah, among other things, schools, the like … tryna get a temperature of the political scene, that kinda deal," I half mumbled, fearing I'd overplayed my hand in my first conversation.

The moose lowered himself off the stool and put a couple of bills on the counter to tip the waitress behind it. The old boy, in a far more delicate and methodical fashion, brought himself down from his stool. I'm not gonna lie, I wasn't entirely sure how this would go for me. The moose placed a big, padded hand on my shoulder.

"You wanna know how people feel 'bout that stuff, check out a site started local, it's called *Stormbarn*. Plenty folks members and that."

The moose and the old boy left like a bizzaro *Of Mice and Men*. The waitress behind the counter topped up my coffee, and I got out my phone to check out the site. The page before me did look remarkably homemade, and I could not congratulate its subtlety enough.

STORMBARN
A BREEDING GROUND FOR PATRIOTS!!!

There wasn't all that much on the site in terms of specifics. In fact, most contributors to this site couldn't quite decide what they thought of the 44th President. On one single page, there was an article that claimed the President was worse than Al-Queda, beneath that was an article that claimed he was in cahoots with Al-Queda, then the article beneath that claimed he was, in fact, the spiritual successor to Hitler. I had doubts Al-Queda, Hitler and a Black guy from Chicago would get on so good, but that was just my ten cents' worth.

The website had a pitch-black background with bold white font bursting from its every single article. None of the articles were particularly long. They were more like rants in list form on subjects which the author was pretty upset about. It read like fan fiction of children who hadn't yet worked out *the more you wish something does not correlate with that thing's ability to occur*. Most glaringly, the articles didn't cover things that had happened or were happening, but things that the author believed might happen one day, apparently.

"Potential FEMA camp next door?
How to check your land for warning signs."
"If the Federal Government takes your guns, next stop:
your home, your babies, your car keys."
"No medical, underpaid, tired of immigrants?
How one tax cut can save all!"

I was nearing the end of my coffee when a dull, invisible, internal kick hit my head. The whole diner tilted and rotated despite the fact I sat still on the spot. Alas, when was the last time I slept?

6

BEFORE MY EYES OPENED MY ears rang with the hum of crickets. My eyes came to in a mid-afternoon sun surrounded by wind-rustled tall grass. There was a beautiful glow on, and I felt easy to continue sleeping, yet as my senses returned, it dawned on me I'd once again woken without meaning to have fallen asleep. I was at a bus shelter a few miles down the road from where the meeting of the county treasurer was happening. No, I did not choose to sleep at a bus shelter. I'd asked the waitress serving at the diner where the nearest motel was. I needed sleep, I needed to lie down, I needed to close my eyes and rest. Even the waitress commented I looked like I could "use a rest."

Some guy named Ned with a bright-red pickup and a confederate flag on his bumper offered to give me a lift to the motel. Ned was stern-faced, and I couldn't see his eyes through his shades. He had a Winchester just behind his seat and occasionally spat a ferocious loogie out of his window. Ned offered me "dip" from a readily available tin of his, I declined "dip," I did not want "dip." He also had an interesting piece of reading literature lying up on the dashboard. Slightly warn and tattered but clearly visible was the front cover of a magazine titled *Packin'*. A giant blow-up image of an assault rifle next to a giant blow-up image of a bullet made up the front cover. Ned was focused on the road; I took a delicate flick through the inside, fascinated.

"Small and compact, but packing power, how to perform with your weapon ..."
"Proven: The longer the barrel, the further the spray ..."
"Get the best out of play, with your 'fun gun' ..."

Ned had interesting reading habits. That being said, he was warm to me, and I made it to the motel in one piece: southern hospitality.

I am yet to find a part of America where the moment you place foot on the site of a motel, the entire world doesn't turn lifeless and grey. Like the motel where you find yourself might be the place you were meant to die. Compared to previous motel experiences though, this one did have a degree of upkeep. The older couple running the place clearly took pride in making sure it looked somewhat respectable. None of the windows had taped over cracks and, to be frank with you, they looked cleaned. An island mound of grass separating parking spaces was the only sign of nature anywhere near. From the lot, the view of the accommodation was a long stretch of first-floor rooms with red fabric curtains blocking a look inside. Undercover from the canopy of the main entrance, I could see the front desk through the glass of the front doors.

The main reception to my eyes was a wooden-walled tiny enclave of a room. Half of it was paneled off with a glass screen, and behind the glass sat a guy behind the front desk. His head was leaning in to the local paper he'd brought about two inches from his face. The "Costanza horse shoe" was his sporting of baldness, and he had his lips pressed together in a grimace. I was in the midst of observing him when he turned to look at me. He leaned his head out beyond his paper and gave me a thousand-yard squint. Before I knew it he'd waddled his way out of his booth and leaned out of the entrance door.

"We got a room just cleaned 'f you're interested?"

The moment I opened my room door and walked inside, a vicious aroma of insecticide told me I probably wouldn't be sleeping.

The lamp on the bedside didn't work, so I closed the door and lay flat on the bed in darkness. The mattress was not so much "hard" as when I lay down it seemed to punch me in the back. Staring at the cork ceiling above me, I noticed the old pattern that led me to a sleepless existence. I could turn off my body, but I couldn't quite turn off my mind. Even at a point where my body was flat, done and felt like it had the weight of a thousand rocks upon it, my mind rattled with a vengeance. Boredom drove me, but I figured I should get back on the PR again. I hit the Twitter account.

> *The Second Amendment stands as our Constitution stands, the price cannot be the fall of our children.*
> *#SaveLivesSaveGuns #BelieveAmerica*

> *Exceptionalism and the abject can never go hand in hand, overcoming our gun violence can awaken our greatness.*
> *#BelieveAmerica*

> *The Founders saw light in every American—our Constitution exists to embolden that, not smother it in senseless violence.*
> *#SLSG #BA*

> *The Second Amendment was meant to assure the homestead's sanctity, not bring lines of grieving parents.*
> *#SaveLivesSaveGuns #BelieveAmerica*

> *Partisanship is the ugliest of privilege. What's broken needs mending. Let's make schools safe again.*
> *#BelieveAmerica #SLSG*

The motel was quiet and it smelled; I wanted to get out. Before I moved on, I showered to at least try to be washed if not rested. Having watered myself like a failing houseplant, I was increasingly becoming restless and made the mistake of taking in my surroundings. The wood of the bed headboard looked dangerously thin. Even the walls of the room looked dangerously thin. Not an article of my room belonged to this decade, or the last three. I had to escape.

I padded along the crusty maroon carpets of the hallway to the reception. I let the gentleman running the place behind his glass little shield know I would be unlikely to return. Before I knew it, I'd been walking a couple of hours down the road till I found a bus shelter. There was always a wander in me. I was never put off by a walk, the longer, the better; I don't know why. There was nothing but the tall grass of the fields around me. Endless blades of green all around me and a stretch of road cutting through. Arriving at the shelter, I took a seat to rest my legs, at least that was my intention.

It was the growl of a pickup's engine that had woken me. A cobalt blue pickup truck filled my line of vision the moment I opened my eyes. The back was filled with men seated, but they looked like they were going to a war zone. Every one of them was covered in body armor or tactical vests; a couple of guys even had bandoliers. Every one of them had tactical shades on, and every one of them had a big ass gun in their hands. The passenger door at the front opened, and a long leg draped in signature blue denim appeared.

As the door opened fully, a tall, ripped figure in a tight black t-shirt tucked into his jeans stepped before me. He like the others had an AR-15 in his hands, specialist shades on and a utility belt with no less than two handguns in it. His face was a picture: stretched, hard skin browned by the sun and a jaw oscillating from chewing gum. A stern, still face glared right at me, decorated with short, white, wire hair up top. For the sake of my heart rate or not, he lowered the gun to hanging beside his leg and pointing at the floor.

"Names Mike. What you doin' out here, partner?"

"Uh, well, I ain't had much sleep. What's the time?"

"Times 5:40 by my makin'. So whatya doin' out here?"

"I'm uh, tryin' make my way to the county treasurer meetin'."

"Is that so? Well, there ain't no buses runnin' in the next twenty, so figure you gonna be late to the meetin'."

"Ah shit."

"We're headin' to the meetin' if you wanna ride?"

I looked at the pick-up truck ready burst into downtown Fallujah. I'd read *Grapes of Wrath* one time; I figured I'd let the my faux Southern twang flow through me.

"Yeh, a'ight."

Squashed between Alan and Mike in the front of the pickup wasn't how I had imagined it would go. Alan was the driver. He had the shiniest head I ever saw and arms the size of my thighs. Every time he pulled the gear stick, I was impaled a foot backward into my seat. Mike sat man-spread like a monsoon of blowjobs was imminent. The sound of his gum bouncing round his mouth and the wind sailing past the car windows was the predominant company on this journey. Alan's tree trunk arm changed gear to forth, and I thought my lung collapsed, then my mouth ran away again.

"Say fellas, what's all the guns for? Is everything OK at the county treasurer's office?"

Alan let out a grunt in his seat. I was fearful his arm would eat me whole.

"Everything's fine at the county treasurer's office 'cus we're keepin' it that way," Mike declared. That sounded nothing but foreboding to me, so I did a dumb thing by saying three words.

"Tell me more."

"We had a likeminded soul make his way round these local counties and across some other states and—"

"He told it like it is," Alan interjected. Honestly, I did not know Alan could talk.

"You know common law?" Mike continued.

"Um … basic stuff, I'm not well versed."

"Common law and common law courts. Why they're the only sovereign law in the United States. All this Federal Government hullabaloo is about keeping people scared and controlled and it ain't even anywhere near the Constitution. That's why they doin' all that sick shit, the bombings, the killings, false flags. See, under the Constitution, the county sheriff's office is the highest form of government the framers had envisaged. Meaning, the Federal

Government's nothing short of illegal GODDAMN IT! Federal Government's a lie, and its creating bad things and there's a 'big day' ahead."

"What 'big day'?"

"Oh there's a 'big day'."

"What happens on the 'big day'?"

"One can never know what will happen on the 'big day'."

"So all the guns are for the 'big day'?"

"These guns could be used on the 'big day'."

"So is today the 'big day'?"

"Today could be the 'big day'."

"What if today isn't the 'big day'?"

"Then we don't use the guns."

I couldn't help but feel Mike's logic was the same as getting all your teeth removed because *'you never know.'* We changed gear again, and I probably broke three ribs. As I prayed to Christ that it wasn't the 'big day', Mike cleaned the metallic bastard in his lap as he continued his manifesto.

"We show up anytime there's anything to do with the county office. We aren't there for trouble, we're there for the protection of ordinary Americans. We don't know what this President is about. We don't. But I do know what I'm seeing. I'm seeing plenty of Iraqis—"

"Ain't they Syrians?" Alan inquired.

"WE GOT SYRIANS OVER HERE NOW???"

I was scared Mike might blow a cap in the roof just to express himself. Instead, he did some weird, shaking, stomping, growling thing; *when lycanthropy meets constipation.* I sat right next to him and between that and Alan's gear changes I felt my life expectancy dropping by the second. Mike composed himself, then began a soliloquy of unbridled unbridledness.

"Either way. What happened to this country 2008 weren't right. Now we got floods of foreigners comin in. Floods of them. I don't buy 2011, Usama Bin Laden ain't dead. I seen him body poppin' on YouTube for christsakes! We've got to protect ourselves now, 'cus we don't know. We don't know what will happen. These fellas comin' round the counties, they been tellin us about a New World Order for years."

"Years *upon* years," Alan added, like a '50s Hausfrau complimenting her husband's gripe.

"All these foreigners, that's what's tearing this country down. They ain't American, this ain't their country and there's so goddamn many of them, why I see them on the news all the time! More than we even know are here, I reckon. We don't know what we don't know. We don't know how much we don't know about what we don't know when we don't know! There's goddamn floods upon floods of these aliens, floods of biblical proportions and that ain't in the Constitution! We didn't say take everybody from everywhere every time! This President don't care and all these freeloadin' aliens are *ruining America!!!* Why my Great Grandaddy came over here a Czech-Swiss-Turk-Albanian; *HE knew what America was about!!!*"

7

THE COUNTY TREASURER'S MEETING WAS fascinating; it ended in five minutes flat. It all kicked off when one lady with round, clear-framed spectacles under a perm of curly grey hair stood up and tearfully proclaimed, "The President's an ... *A-rab!*" The entire town hall exploded into blind panic. Within a second there was a flurry of screaming and running in different directions. Some guys figured jumping at closed windows was as good as using the open doors. One fella towards the back with a pencil moustache and a tragic combover yelled across the ruckus, "WOMEN AND CHILDREN FIRST!" He then ran out before any of the women and children. I found myself leaned up against the back wall, and the sight was incredible. People were hurdling over people and pulling them towards the exits like soldiers dragging wounded comrades in war. I was perfectly content taking in the opera of pointlessness, when a skinny bug-eyed guy leapt towards me yelling, "*SAVE YOURSELF!!*" How he thought I was meant to save myself hoisted over *his* shoulder, I still don't know.

Outside the town hall, once Buscemi on PCP put me down, there were people sprinting in all directions away from the hall. In the grey gravel of the parking lot, Mike and Alan and the "Sooner Mens Militia" were the only party with any form of calm, whatsoever. After cracked Buscemi had bearhugged me off the ground and tearfully whimpered, "God *save America*," I carefully made my way over to the blue pick-up. The rhythm of Mike's gum had not

changed since the journey over. Most of the guys in the back of
the pick-up seemingly hadn't moved since I first laid eyes on them.
Mike had a wry smile on his face, his row of whitened teeth nearly
matching his bright, light hair. "Happens every other Thursday.
Needent worry. At least we know they're prepared."

"Prepared? You mean for the 'big day'?"

"No, in case of a fire, ya idiot!"

Mike and Alan lumbered about scowling at anything in the
nearby vicinity, only to be interrupted by occasional loving gazes
at their guns. They soon informed me what I had witnessed was a
phenomenon known as "Obamagrief." It was a brutal sensation that
had riddled states across the south. The more fondly you remembered *Birth of a Nation*, the harder it hit ya. By Mike's reckoning,
the mutiny before us would all return after approximately 40 minutes, but they needed a good half hour or so of wild flailing and
frantically reciting Psalms.

When it was just myself and the guys and the abandoned town
hall, I continued my field op and persuasion work as we put all the
chairs back in place. Mike and Alan took me deadly seriously and
"thanked God" there was "someone out in DC protecting guns."
I could not say I understood, got, or would support these guys, but
we found agreement that children should not be getting shot in
schools or for that matter, anywhere. I gave them the relevant flyers, then with the militia's blessing I placed a flyer on every single
seat of the empty town hall. I knew I didn't have any intention
of staying, and Mike said he'd even put in a quick word for me.
Despite me never saying anything of the sort, Mike declared I had
"recognized the importance of the Militia's role." Recruitment, who
would have guessed?

I made off down the road. It was a little out in the country;
long winding roads, shimmering fields and a woozy sunset were all
that was ahead of me. My main concern was getting any kind of
phone signal back, which I hadn't had since the motel. Along my
way, I came across a huge college-age guy who must have been from
the town hall meeting, his arms were all bruised from the failed

window dives. He was slumped on the side of the road, sat with his legs folded on the ground as he sobbed. He looked like a spiritually flatlined Buddha. His mop of light brown hair, pubic beard and flannel—

This was the guy who tipped me off to the meeting; it was the moose philosopher king. Since he got me involved with this demographic, I felt like I owed him somewhat, somehow. I felt bad instantly seeing him sat in the dirt like that. I stopped right by him and tried to interact with him. His head didn't raise but his shoulders kept jumping with consistent sobbing. He was leaned forward with his big chunky hand supporting his fallen head. Through a cracking, tear-tightened voice he mumbled in defiance, "Ain't gettin' me eatin' hummus ya sumbitch. *Ain't gettin' me eatin' hummus!*" I feared the day he'd hear of baba ghanoush.

By the time my phone signal returned it was dark out and I was still marching along the side of the road like a nomad. When I finally got enough bars to refresh my inboxes and get online, it was a flat minute of continual bleating from my phone. Mainly from Andros.

Hey dude, this PAC isn't a joke, get back to me.
Andros

Sam, this is getting some real momentum, get back to me. P.S is that you on the Twitter account?
Andros

Sam, it's Andros, do you like things that are green? Because there's a lot coming in here dude. Get back to me.
Andros

Sam, when you said I'd be treasurer, I didn't think I'd handle this amount of money, pick up your phone man.
Andros

*FOR CHRISTSAKE SAM! PICK UP YOUR PHONE!
WE'VE GOT THREE QUARTERS OF A GODDAMN
MILLION HERE, AND I DON'T KNOW WHAT THE
HELL WE'RE DOING WITH IT!!??*
Andros

I also received an email from Natalie.

Sam,
Are you like, off from work again? Let me know, I'll pass on
the word.
N

I was out in the country and it was dark and a chill was set-ting in. I had reached the point of no sleep where your eyes start watering any time they please. Usually with a sharp lasting sting that coats your eye sockets. I couldn't even tell at the time how long I'd been out in Oklahoma. I thought it was a day or two, but I could have been way off. Infrequent car headlights and the sound of crickets were my only guide in the darkness. I don't know how long it was before I managed to get a ride back to Oklahoma City Airport.

Sitting in the front passenger seat, my body gave off an un-comfortable tightness on the skin and a cringy feeling of grime all over. The hum of the engine and the cats eyes along the road felt like a form of punishment, a purgatory conveyor belt I couldn't escape. Three quarters of a million? I remember thinking at the time … what was I gonna do with all this money? I didn't have an immediate answer. My logic and lack of options led me to phone Andros and assure him to keep the ship running. He informed me that the Office of the Secretary of the Senate had been in contact; they wanted to know where all this money was going. I told him it would be handed on to the relevant parties after successful pitching to the donor classes. I then told him to tell them that.

I was trying to get comfortable in my seat when Darleen, the driver kind enough to give me a ride, began talking about her cats.

It turns out Darleen lived with over 14 cats. Darleen was looking forward to returning to her cats. Darleen found her cats to be
"real characters." Darleen was giddy with excitement about returning to them. Darleen needed to find out if her feline friends had
left her any "little brown bears" for her to clean up. Darleen had
novelist-level backstories for each one of the cats and audiobook
standards of storytelling. The Feline-a Monologues showed no sign
of abating; I felt safer in the front of the pick-up with Alan and
Mike, and the airport couldn't arrive soon enough.

At this point I have only three memories of reference. One in
the airport departures lounge lolling my head around involuntarily,
thanks to a body not sure if it should be awake or asleep. A strange
one on a plane, where I have a plastic cup of orange juice in my
upright hand despite laying near flat. Then my last memory that I
can recall was looking down into my melatonin delivery back in my
DC shoebox, my hands reaching into the stacks of small card med
boxes. From what I have been told and can understand in retro-
spect, at this point, I slept. Oh boy, did I sleep.

Apparently if you sleep for two weeks flat that medically could
be regarded as a coma. It should be explained I did somewhat
overdo the melatonin dosage. I just gobbled down several packs.
In my defense, when your eyes sting anytime you blink or, for that
matter, keep them open, *reading the instructions* is not your deal.
Waking up was quite a remarkable thing because my eyes opened
and my body simply could not move. I left consciousness half
slumped to the right while sitting up with my head fallen forward
on the couch. My chemical-induced slumber was so heavy I hadn't
moved an inch in two weeks. It was like waking up encased in a
marble statue and a really crap one at that. I called a chiropractor
but first I had to wash and change the golem I'd become. I may have
been out for the count for two weeks but my bowels had not.

The bell to my apartment rang and I awkwardly staggered to
the door and opened it. A young Latina face appeared. Her eyes
lit up like Las Vegas upon seeing me. The young lady did not enter my apartment, but fearfully inquired: "How can I help you?"
I explained the situation and what had happened. Martina didn't

respond, she only nodded with eyes like golf balls. When I finished the explanation she asked: "Are you in pain right now sir?"

"Oh, yeah."

"You don't need a chiropractor; you need a hospital."

Martina was sweet; she stayed with me till the ambulance arrived, even when I told her she didn't have to. We stood in the doorway, sitting was just as uncomfortable as standing. Furthermore, while I took no pride in being a sub-par host, I kind of needed to buy a new couch.

8

I WASN'T ACTUALLY TRANSFERRED TO A hospital. The medic took one look at me and gave a simple: "Oh boy."

The ambulance took me instantly to the National Spine and Pain Center just off Dupont Circle. This was my place of residence for the coming month. The process of having your spine realigned and straightened, I honestly wouldn't advise. The whole experience strikes me as a blur of palms, knees, slings and god-awful crunching sounds. By the time I left, there was not a single involuntary sound I could make that the staff had not heard. All things considered, the staff were excellent and professional, and the dosages of painkillers I was eventually given were wonderful.

It was about a week into the stay when, each day, a line of medical students would arrive. They asked me questions and my given answers would light up their faces like I'd just completed their thesis for them. On reflection, they were particularly interested in exactly how I'd done this to myself. They usually came in traditional coats and lanyards; they were pretty feverish note takers. A handful of times, particularly enthusiastic medical students would try poking me or putting pressure on this or that part of my back. It did nothing but they seemed to have a good time.

The main thing I took from the month at the Center was when they brought in the sleep specialist. For about three or four days, a short and direct-speaking woman with a harsh mole on her forehead came and told me all about it. Her name was Magda, and everything she said freaked me out. According to Magda (yes there was a Polish accent and yes, I quite liked it), there's someone dying per hour in the US due to a fatigue-induced driving error. She said that 56 million Americans had stated they found it hard to stay awake behind the wheel each month. That works out to about a quarter of a million per day falling asleep behind the wheel. I told Magda I didn't drive. She was taken aback the moment I said it.

"You had car accident?"

"No."

"Then … how this happen to your back?"

"I slept funny."

"Figures."

Magda's delivery was punctuated by her left arm karate chopping at certain words for emphasis. Hard Polish dialect cased a series of far from soft messages. That no major psychiatric illness showed normal sleep hygiene. That basic brain functions like memory retention and emotional stability were eroded by poor sleep. She said sleep deprivation is a sure way to bring on anhedonia. She told me anhedonia is when you cannot get pleasure from anything pleasurable. I thought what Magda called anhedonia most called marriage.

Magda soon informed me that, if I continued with my current patterns of sleeping, I'd 200 percent increase my chances of having a stroke or a coronary. She told me that, once I'd passed 45, such sleeping patterns were gravely consequential. When I told Magda I wasn't 45 yet, not only did Magda not laugh, she looked like she wanted to hit me. Maybe she sensed she was dealing with some form of idiot, but Magda's tone softened. She started to talk to me like I was eight; all she wanted was for me to sleep and I wanted that too. Between us, we decided that getting me a regular sleep pattern down was probably the best plan. Magda was extremely specific and clear about the correct dosages of melatonin. For a contingency, she informed me that an escape to somewhere sunny or remote was a must if all else failed.

When my program was over at the Spine and Pain Center, I had a regimented lifestyle routine to stick to, my "aftercare" program.

My back was delicate and still in some form of recovery. Thanks to work at the Center, my sleep hygiene was better than it had been in months. My priority was establishing routine; Magda had said no changing time zones, no all-nighters. I needed a regular rhythm to my life if sleep were to stay in it. The only things important leaving the Center were getting good sleep, taking my pain killers, doing my physio, and getting back to work. DC looked different to me after all the rehab. It did not look like a place to be; it looked like a place to be swallowed whole.

The stairs in my apartment building kind of held the clue to the months ahead. My walking wasn't exactly at a pace in this immediate aftercare period. I had to take it one step at time with a hand on the stair rail. The only thing that felt missing was a cane. One guy in my building, a young skinny guy called Jack, asked me if "I needed help." I'd only see Jack going on or coming back from a run. I turned down his offer and slowly made my way up to my apartment door. My lower back didn't hurt, yet it felt like it could burst into a state of pain at any moment. Putting my keys in my front door for the first time, I felt supreme relief.

My apartment looked a little sterile. Midday light barely made its way into the shoebox, and it had the look of a place abandoned. While its aura did nothing for me, the shoebox smell was a much worse conundrum. Memory only prompted me the moment I'd returned, but I hadn't managed to clean up the clothes or replace the couch in which I'd sleep-shat myself. The only immediate solution was to make a huge pillow-adorned nest on my bed. By the time I was finished constructing the cotton haven, I was near grateful I had a back injury to excuse it. The pillow haven looked and felt regal and most importantly, with a mild dose of painkiller, I could sleep on it.

The think tank was kind of exceptional about my circumstances. Once again, I could come and go as I pleased, and that meant working around my physio and rehab. Waking on my pillow nest, I would begin my day with my stretches and exercises. I had let Natalie know what had happened to my back. She replied in an email suggesting a small repertoire of yoga stuff that really helped. During the first mornings after the stay, I wasn't even touching coffee. My accident had left me a helpless pillar of goodwill upon my body. Thanks to my insurance plan I could get Ubers to and from work as it went into aftercare considerations for my back. Work itself however became only initial comfort.

Returning to the basement was a pleasure. As I made my way down the steps to the office/tank door, I could hear Natalie and the guys chatting the breeze. When I opened the door, I was greeted warmly but had to ward off any hugs on the grounds of my back. My swivel chair had gone and instead in my place was some gorgeous big armchair, a few decades old. It did look photoshopped in the basement the moment I sat in it, however it worked wonders for my back. A few weeks in sitting back down at my workspace, I was told one thing.

"The AFT aren't playing around ..."

In my weeks away, the teachers of America were making abundantly clear the conditions our children faced were urgent. Instead of compiling a report based on metrics, they'd logged actual teachers giving on the ground accounts. So began a long process of detailing every account and trying to synthesize the themes in what I was reading. "Who" from "where" was pointing out "problem A" as opposed to "problem B, C or D." I had moments—sifting through lines of text, taking down notes and drawing up the grander picture—where I felt determined. As the work went on though, the shadow of knowing that change wasn't arriving anywhere soon had a weight to it.

A teacher in north Detroit said that the middle and elementary school libraries hadn't received a budget in over four years. Out in Aurora, Colorado, a teacher spoke of teaching 25 children in a trailer the size of a hotel room, colloquially called a "mobile classroom." An elementary school teacher out in Texas made clear how classroom budgets had dropped to $200. There was some smart cookie out in Boston who surveyed his colleagues´ and his own out-of-pocket expenses in a year; it hit over $25,000.

My sad sandwiches had returned to the Mall much like myself. After a particularly long day of staring the bleak in the eye, I sat on the Mall zoned out and feeling somewhat hollow. I was pleasantly surprised when Natalie came to join me one time. Natalie was not equipped with a sad sandwich; she had some hyper health wrap concocted with seeds, kale, and lentils. All the super health stuff I respected from a distance, but I'd turn narcoleptic whenever it came near me. Maybe that was the way to get me sleeping again, just walk into the center of Whole Foods and pass out.

Natalie had been seated for a few minutes and was a couple of bites into her wrap when she asked,

"Whatcha doin?"

"Eating lunch, how did you find me?"

"Everyone knows you eat out here."

"Yeah?"

"Yeah, with your little sandwich."

"What do people think?"

"Oh, they think you're weird."

"Oh. You don't think I'm weird right?"

"I didn't say that."

"Oh."

We sat in relative silence for a little bit, then my mouth ran away again.

"What the fuck are we doing here, man?"

"Wow, wow, where's this come from?"

"Look at what we're reading here."

"Oh, I do."

"What is it now? The spending deficit for schools?"

"Exact figures ... ah, doesn't matter, point is; it won't get a chance to be changed till it grows to $1.3 trillion."

"Then what are we even doing here, man?"

"What do you mean?"

I felt myself all full of tears and I don't know why.

"Jesus Christ, rotting ceilings, 25-year-old text books—I mean, shit, we're all complaining about the state of the roads and the trains and the fuckin' railways. We've got children sitting in buildings not renovated since the interwar period, using dried up marker pens for 'art.' This isn't an education system, this is a charade pretending to be one. This is some form of disgrace, pure and simple. The state of Congress means we can't even get close to an answer on this."

I had a near growl in my voice. Natalie had stopped eating; I guess I wasn't all that appetizing.

"This is how we've set this up. The state of things didn't happen overnight or rise up from under the ground like Lovecraft. We left the state of our children's environments to rot and fester ... and we did it in a way that the term 'accountability' can be an item of suspicion, particularly our own, and we did this over decades. You know what anyone would say if they saw all these decisions and choices on paper? They'd say America doesn't give a shit about its children."

Natalie took a deep inhale.

"If it's any good to you, in the some of these schools we've got metal detectors and teachers armed with mace. Nothing speaks of love for the kids like preparing to mace 'em!"

Natalie's sardonic tone didn't do all that much for me. I didn't finish my sandwich and sat there in a profound huff. Natalie observed me; she giggled. I think I realized what was behind Natalie's warmth towards me: I made the afternoons go quicker.

"It's OK to be bummed out some days, dude. You've done this kind of stuff for years though, right? You know the game, you know the real picture of this place is always harder to stomach than the one we're taught to dream."

She paused a moment.

"Although, metal detectors in schools, that's uh, that's an all-American one, my friend."

Natalie picked up the end of wrap and delicately placed it in her mouth; she then less delicately declaimed,

"FURKED URRRRP."

Natalie got up, dusting any wrap figments off her leggings.

"See ya inside, dude. And er ... don't break your back over this."

As she headed back in the direction of our beloved basement, a wave of florid anxiety washed over me. The metal detectors, of course, a visual reminder every Monday morning your classmates could be pre-disposed to kill you. The guns … in my rehab mode, I'd got close to forgetting I'd even started a PAC and, well, a movement of sorts. I could be a fool, I could be the kind of idiot who just can't help but tempt nature, I could do things that were not good for me. So, I got out my phone. I checked my relevant inboxes.

On that given day, I had one email forwarded on to me from Andros. The heading of the email was an emoji. The emoji that looks like it's been informed its childhood pet died. Andros had forwarded me an email from the Office of the Secretary of the Senate. It was a second warning; the email made clear they hadn't exactly been impressed by my first response to them. They wanted official references on behalf of the parties where the money would be going. It was pretty stern in tone, the wording was stretching into the litigative, and I had a deadline on my hands. If I couldn't provide what they wanted when they wanted, I was due an official investigative interview from them. Jesus.

9

THAT AFTERNOON, MY DESK CONTENTS—A borderline greasy keyboard surrounded by stacks of paper—stared back up at me. Cornered by further claims of entrenched educators, I could hardly bring myself back to task. The swivel in my chair had been taken away but the tapping of my feet returned. The cool blue of the basement walls and the rattling of keyboards told me everyone was busy. Assured by the distraction of others, I delved into researching lobbyists. I needed a lobbyist. If there was one kind of bastard who'd do anything for me in the name of money, it was a lobbyist.

DC has notorious hotspots filled with congressmen (and every twenty years, a congresswoman or two …) ankle deep in their own sweat. In DC, all you need to do is walk into the tackiest-looking seafood place available, and you'll find "respectable leaders" begging for money. I looked online for any place local that served shrimp and found one. Its profile photo suggested the late-'70s had never died, and there was an all you can eat $8.98 shrimp buffet. This sounded like the perfect environment to find fully grown adults degrading their standards by the second. I had my plan for the end of work.

The canopy outside the joint said it all. Green material displayed the printed white font of "Patricks Seafood Shack." However, most of the letters had faded, leaving only, "PiSS." The windows visible from the front were foggy with steam. A palm slapped flat against the inside one of the steamed windows; it was just like the scene in *Titanic*, but the hand had a wad of dollars in it. Opening the entrance door unleashed a plume of gaseous substance and I couldn't be sure of the contents. It smelled a little bit like a shrimp fry; it smelled a little bit like a locker room; it smelled a bit like printed money; and it smelled a bit like when people's dignity dies.

Inside was a moderately sized space with scores of tables packed full of people. The chairs looked like they'd been inherited from the hotel in *The Shining*, and the white tablecloths had seafood stains all over. There was a congressman standing at the far end of the restaurant with a microphone. He was a round man with a smile so fixed it was disturbing. His egg-like head had a thick coat of sweat cascading off it. His light-blue shirt had turned navy with perspiration. As his hand shook visibly with the microphone, he tried to connect with his crowd.

"Well ... the thing about estate tax ..."

My usual routine of occupying the back and observing proceedings took hold. The tables mainly comprised overweight white dudes arguing over who had met Elon Musk or Warren Buffett most recently. One table got particularly animated when two such gentlemen began rowing over the exact decimal net worth of Jeff Bezos. They rose to their feet (revealing braces holding up their pants ...) and began dueling their empty lobster shells. The two behemoths began circling around one another with seafood giblets hanging from the mouths. It sorta looked like a T-Rex mating ritual.

I kept an eye on the tables and the chatter but particularly on the lobbyists working the room, going round each table. The lobbyists were the sharpest dressed in the room and had become the personal maître d' for every table. Listening to the way the guys spoke, it didn't make sense; they were way too cozy in the name of money. A red tie on a pinstripe grey suit spoke to one table like he was their family doctor. A mauve tie under a dark grey suit was asking questions only a fiduciary should ask. A green tie finishing a royal blue suit was squatting down, her hand in his, hearing out a wife's concern over her husband's spending. Boy, did these guys make me wanna scream.

The dry, elastic panging of gum between teeth caught my attention. There was a presence standing to my left on the back wall. I only slightly turned my head, to get a check in my periphery. The suited man, like a jackal, stopped chewing the moment I did this. In my periphery I saw him looking at me in his periphery. It was the creepiest moment of all time. When I went back to scanning the room, the gum continued to be chewed. His presence was still; I felt kind of hunted and I didn't want to move. A gravelly dark voice arrived.

"So you like what the congressman is bringing to the table?"

"I couldn't give a shit about the congressman. How long has this been going on for?"

"This fundraiser?"

"Yeah."

"Since last March. We started with around 140 donors in here but about a third didn't make it. We sent on condolences to all the families concerned."

"They died?"

"I prefer to say they gave their lives for something they believe in."

"Holy shit."

He turned in a near pirouette to take up my vision entirely, face to face.

"What can I do for you today?"

"Look, before I decide whether to work with you, tell me about yourself, tell me who you work for."

"I work on a contracted-out, not-for-profit, grassroots, top-down, government-approved private consultancy, to do the relevant inter-locking between investors and clients."

"So, sorry, who do you work for?"

"I provide service on a strategist advisory specialist basis on behalf of contracting enterprise. What can we make happen here today?"

"You, you didn't … who do you work for?"

"State entities broker great gains in the work we do as a private commodity."

"WHO DO YOU WORK FOR???!?!"

"Non-access engagement, industry-standard operating provided on intra-financed state private practices."

"Oh Christ, just tell me what you *actually do* …"

"Monitoring logistical transactor—"

"SIRI ON ACID, I GET IT! I have *money*, alright??!"

The jackal paused to lick his lips and gave a micro scowl to the entire restaurant. Then he leaned into me.

"Keep talking."

"We're about to hit the million mark, our following is dedicated and show no signs of slowing."

"What do you wanna do with it?"

"I've got a solid earner, alright?"

"Earning in what?"

"Got a solid earner in … property insurance and medical insurance."

"Solid earner? In both?"

"Yeah."

The jackal eased. In fact, the jackal's entire presence and stance softened. I looked at his face; it was like I was his kid saying "I love you" on Father's day.

"Buddy. You must be some kind of fuckin' genius."

The jackal snapped his fingers up in the air hurriedly, then bellowed across the room: "PATRON! We're gonna need 4 screwdrivers here!"

Over the screwdrivers, the jackal informed me his name was Adam. Adam was quick to get out his wallet and show me pictures of his wife and children. He then informed me he saw them about ten times a decade. Adam seemed great in comparison to the jackal, and the more screwdrivers I drank, the more the two seemed like different people. Adam was ferocious in his enthusiasm, and I realized this was the first person I had met who'd actively encouraged my idea.

Adam assured me everything was on him. He said that, when the insurance companies heard where these expenses were going, they'd be happy to hear them spent. Adam whisked me away from the euthanasia fish sweat box to one of the most expensive restaurants in DC. You know the ones: all the interior is decorated with odd shapes suspended in air, either cool metallic or gold, and the portions tend to be the size of your fingernail. By the time we got seated in a rounded, felt, corner booth, I had a bit of a blur going. Between the alcohol and the pain killers and the company, none of this quite looked good. Also, I'm not sure of this, but I may have been dribbling.

Adam's perfectly combed, greying hair, sun-bleached redness and cigar-stained voice was coming right at me. Like any on the plateau of donor class, "surf and turf" seemed to be some universal tribute to wealth and power. Adam was no exception. He tore through his lobster like it was bread; I glanced at its face a moment—it was perhaps the saddest crustacean I ever saw. Trying to sober up and keep consciousness, I stuck to the bread on the table. Adam's odd face burst into an illicit smile the moment money got mentioned. The red wine flowed and so did Adam's tales, about Adam.

He informed me he'd been working since the early '90s. Doing what and for whom was still an incredibly difficult detail to get off him. Adam worked government. Then Adam worked private. Then Adam worked government. Then Adam worked private. According to Adam, that was in just the first eighteen months of his work. He said his role and expertise leant itself to "anti-transparency" and that the GAO did nothing but "slow things down." When I asked what the GAO was, Adam's face flourished again and he declared,

"This is what I like working with."

The glow of the restaurant maybe sank me; maybe I should have asked more and done more. I do remember asking Adam, if he ever worried that bouncing so much between private and government might produce conflicts of interest. Adam was still equipped with his big ol' words, three bottles of red and seven screwdrivers in. After sucking the meat from the lobster's ass shell, Adam said, "Fluid non-performance ad-hoc communality engagement shows net profitability." He fired off a belch that knocked over a waiter, and I still didn't know what the fuck he was talking about.

It was night out by the time we were finishing up at our table. Adam had signed off on everything. He was happy to be my referee and go between for funds raised for the PAC. He told me he had been in contact with the Senates office countless times doing this kind of work. Adam was particularly enthused to get us up to the eight-figure mark. Adam reckoned we could draw in tens of millions. My head was spinning and I needed to get back to the shoebox. I stood to send off Adam, and he rose to meet me too. I noticed Adam had the shoes of an Italian count; somebody didn't mind spending.

I had always heard that you *should not* mix anti-depressants and alcohol. Sitting in the Uber riding home, I couldn't remember if that applied to painkillers and alcohol. The streetlights of DC were smudged blurs passing by me defenseless in the back of the taxi. When we pulled up at a place, turned out that was my building and I flopped out of the car door. I clawed my way back to my feet and swayed up the building steps. Making my way through the building stairs to my apartment was more like shitty dodgems; I made it up by bouncing off the walls the entire way. After a five-minute struggle of great ferocity over only two keys, I managed to open my apartment door.

Whether it's a territorial thing or not, I don't know, but I find the moment I get back through the front door, I'm usually busting for a piss. That night was no different. I remember swaying my way down the little stretch of hallway to my bathroom. Slamming the door behind me with a sense of victory and close to zero balance, I turned, dropped my pants and plonked myself on the toilet—

THUNDER. SEARED. THROUGH. MY. SPINE.

To be frank, I stopped breathing for a full half minute. It was a long, long half minute; I even got a look at me in the mirror. No one should ever look like that, not even sitting on the toilet. I had no earthly idea what I'd done. Clearly something had flared in my back of such importance that it cut through painkillers and a lot of alcohol. Once I caught my breath, I tried not to move. Initially I was just trying to stay calm. I tried moving from my hips but that felt delicate. I tried stretching my legs but that was much the same.

Then it began. I didn't want it to. It made me feel ill. It was honestly a disturbing moment. Something I was powerless to. Something that was out of my power to stop. I had to move myself. I had to get off the toilet I was seated on. It was the only option available and it just occurred. I couldn't stop it. My back was adjusting itself. I'm a person too, you know? Like I said, I am not proud. This just happened. I couldn't stop it. Please don't judge me.

I started leaning to the right ...

10

Awaking on the pillow haven had lost its joy. Opening my eyes come about 9 was nearly tearful. It wasn't the first time I had opened my eyes over the last few hours. My sleep was heavily disrupted; my constructed mountain of cotton hadn't been able to save me. My given dosage of OxyContin was suddenly proving ineffective; I had to double down just to get me to sitting. I was grateful for the slight blur on feeling that it provided, and I was suddenly able to make decisions. When I made it to the mirror opposite my bed, my lean was visibly evident and I felt adrift.

Rehabilitation had to be my priority. I had to get my back into better health again. It was midweek. I emailed Natalie letting her know my back was tender and I'd be returning at the start of next week. That morning, a hangover to knock out a cow was not helping. My diet for the day was water by the gallon, and the only position I could find close to comfortable was standing. Turning on the TV for some form of company or at least background noise didn't do all that much for me. My eyes had a uncannily familiar sense of dryness to them. Long days were ahead of me.

Being locked indoors in the same location day upon day with no change is not healthy for a person. Maybe that's why all the Presidents were some degree of batshit. Though not a fan of the choice or culture, I did a food shop online. I wanted my back better; I didn't give a shit what it took. Over the next three days, I drank water till it tasted like liquid metal. Threw back supplements like my life literally depended on it. Devoured stacks of spinach, seeds and kale which unfortunately tasted like spinach, seeds and kale. The rehabilitation exercises and work was the hardest though; it wasn't playing and it had consequences.

A mixture of tears and whimpers and growling emanated the moment I did any exercise. Even Natalie's yoga stuff wasn't proving an easy task. The only way I made it through the rehab work was by upping my painkiller dosage. Yes, this was not a good idea. Yes, I'd been told to make sure I informed my doctor if adjusting my dosage. No, I didn't do that. Lo and behold, it well and truly started messing with my sleep. All things considered though, my last chance saloon with my back did wonders for the Twitter account:

> *Only from the depths of the hardest despair can our exceptionalism heal that in need of repair. #BelieveAmerica #SLSG*

> *The protection of our rights does not qualify the abandonment of our young. #BelieveAmerica #SLSG*

> *Schools can be sanctuaries, guns can be respected, our children can be safe and our amendments protected. #SaveLivesSaveGuns #BA*

> *Dreams are not make believe images for fools; they are possibilities that demand the most of us. #SaveLivesSaveGuns #BelieveAmerica*

> *Our compact pledges to provide our youngest the best, how dare we rob them of that which we swore to owe #BelieveAmerica #SaveLivesSaveGuns*

Come Thursday night, I was no longer in love with the shoebox and the haven of pillow. I wanted to get out, but my back was far from agreeing with that sentiment. The single light bulb hanging above my lounge was the only source of light. Shuffling my way over to my windowed wall, I took a glance out to DC at night. A heaviness filled my chest when I thought of my first arrival here upon getting the think tank job. There was a warm memory of marching through the Mall with a sense I'd made a good decision for me, that my life was getting less complicated. Shows how much I fucking know.

My phone rang on the long-abandoned desk in my lounge. It did that aggressive rumbling travel that phones on vibrate do. The one that suggests the phone is having a tantrum. Upon answering, a gravelly voice filled my ear and it could only be Adam. It was difficult to tell over the phone if Adam sounded intrigued, stoned or aroused, but once again his enthusiasm was off the charts. In a matter of days, Adam had managed to secure me access to an investor donor event in California. He asked if I could make it for Saturday night. I knew the one answer I could not give was "yes" but the one answer I couldn't say was "no." I was silent. Adam then said it was a summit for shareholders in insurance with board members in mandatory attendance. I booked my flight.

Strangely enough, my regimen of melatonin and OxyContin had not made sleep less disrupted but reality more so. Come Friday night, I was sitting in the compact uprightness of coach class drugged to my eyeballs on a plane flying West. I had the window seat and the surrounding of thick fluffy clouds was my only reference to some normality. Sitting to my left was a married couple, nearest me, the husband. His face did look legitimately concerned; after some nudging from his wife, he did the dutiful thing of inquiring,

"Are you OK there, buddy?"

I tried speaking. However, it came out very international, just about every dialect on the planet rolled into one. A little bit European, little bit Asian, little bit Middle Eastern and a little bit African.

"Jesuni Abor tep tep irunake. Fimque Onchline?"

It was the last interaction I had with them on that flight. Though I can remember them conferring to each other shortly afterward, the husband started in a stage whisper: "See that's what pisses me off about this country. Why on earth does he not have *some kind* of support worker on this flight with him? Tell me that!"

"OK, OK, don't say it so loud that *he can hear you*," the wife responded urgently.

The rest of the flight to my memory was leaned up against the window. I had an accidental waking snore, and I'm certain some involuntary drooling occurred. As my lolling eyes looked out into the darkness and the occasional passing of clouds, my mind wandered. Magda's voice had returned and it wasn't fun. A Polish angel on my shoulder was full of stern warning. *Just four hours of sleep wipes out 70% of immune cells. Sleep deprivation erodes the synapses of basic memory retention. There are increasing links to poor sleep and the development of Alzheimer's in later life. Physical fitness cannot counter the damage to coronary arteries by sleep deprivation.*

A hefty thump made me wince and announced the plane had landed. My main concern was stopping my jaw from hanging and increasingly looking like a human being. Waddling my way through the cabin was alright. When one of the flight attendants placed her hand on my shoulder and said I was "very brave for flying alone" was a little less so. I knew that the night with the insurance folks was a big shot for me. I knew I could screw it up as well; if we didn't have the insurers on our sides the Save Lives, Save Guns movement was doomed. My wobbling mind was pranging with thoughts of JFK drugged to his eyeballs meeting Khrushchev for the first time. Yet that didn't stop me losing two whole fascinated hours staring at the luggage collection going round.

I was lucky in that Andros was keen to pick me up the moment I'd told him I was heading out to Cali. Outside LAX with the sun blaring on my near vampiric ass, Andros soon pulled up in a prehistoric Datsun. It had unnervingly old suspension, low ride out of wear as opposed to low ride out of design. The passenger door swung open and Andros signaled me in. Upon sitting, the car did lean somewhat to my side. In defense of the car, it was made decades before my time and probably didn't understand "fat shaming."

I looked to my left, and Andros seemed much like he always had: long, dark, almost greasy hair, a patterned flowing over shirt three sizes too big and jeans that looked sprayed on. His face told me he was taken aback.

"Jesus Christ, I've been sitting out here for nearly two hours! Wait, are you even sober?"

"EKUN yesd bellcheip, yuwana!"

"Right," Andros said and drove us out of arrivals and on towards miles of freeway.

Being surrounded by lanes of traffic in the sun did bring me back towards some coherence. Andros was pretty animated, and when he got talking I soon understood why. Getting out my phone to confirm was a glimpse into just how much my sleep mangled state had me missing out on. The Twitter account had begun an ascension all its own. The car seemed to travel in slow motion as I checked but the account had gone from a following of around eighty thousand people to around eight hundred thousand. As the world stayed in slow motion, I looked at Andros once again. We were over half hour into the drive and he had an uncharacteristic nervousness to him.

"The Twitter account, I dunno, I—is that you?"

"Yeeeeee."

"I always asked you why you never did speechwriting. I *always* asked that."

I did the shrug of an idiot instead of more slurring.

"Look, the Twitter account, I get that's in its own universe, sure. Have you seen we now have 2 million in the PAC?"

I let out another idiot's shrug, even if I'd had words, they wouldn't have relayed the anxiety I was feeling. Andros took a left.

"Who is Adam, dude? It's like you've hired the snake from the garden of Eden."

"Eda monjay."

"Wha?"

"Heeeeee laaa Mooo-naaayyyy"

"Money? H—oh, 'he's the money.'"

I gave another big idiot's thumbs up like a make shift *Lassie*.

"OK, well, are you sure you know what you're doing with it?"

I gave a big idiot's nod. Andros pulled into a small suburban drive and what looked like an abandoned house.

"This is us," he said with confidence.

As we walked up the drive and towards the front door, I looked across the concrete lacing the empty drives and open garages. As Andros opened the door, it swept over a swamp of unopened mail. His speechwriting claim wasn't true. One time I did speechwriting for a mayoral candidate out in Wyoming who was looking for someone on short notice. The story was his speechwriter had been hit with "hipster flu," it strikes just as bad as real flu but it *really takes its time*. This speechwriter was supposed to be a college grad but the whiz kid was bedridden. At the time I was scheduler for another campaign out in Portland two weeks away, so I figured "why not?" Never do anything on the grounds of "*why not?*"

The mayoral candidate was a huge pro-life guy. I am not. I am not pro-life but boy oh boy, this guy wanted me to carve out like a full five- to 10-minute stump on the subject. I didn't feel that great on the task, but I knew working in arenas I wasn't comfortable with would only add to my capacity as a political operator. Well that was the plan. I can remember chain smoking round the back of a town hall staring at a creased notepad with my mind as dry as a bone. I had eight hours to come up with something I did not want to write on a subject I did not agree with. The result wasn't what the mayor to be had hoped for. I was making revisions right up to the final moment. I can still remember him reading the opening lines as I looked on from back stage.

"Thank you all for being here. Tonight, let us reap the benefits of *having not been* aborted …"

My speechwriting career was doomed, but so were the mayor's prospects. I could live with that.

Andros' place was the wreck it always promised to be. The organizational skills of a gig musician hadn't left him. Looking up at the ceiling, none of the lights had any bulbs in them. When Andros offered me a drink, he opened a tragically bare fridge, paused briefly then let me know he had, "water" or "water." I accepted water and lowered myself onto a beaten-up brown leather couch that made a startling puncture sound the moment I was seated. Andros took a seat next to me and sunk himself into the wounded veteran of a couch. He slowly placed his feet on the glass coffee table in front of us. Which didn't look like it had been cleaned in a while either.

Andros looked at me. "What's up with you? What is all this?"

I shrugged, unsure what exactly he was referring too.

"You're drooling and you look atrocious and I can't get any sense out of you …"

Like I was translating for the hard of hearing, I informed with my hands and arms to Andros that I'd damaged my back and I'd had trouble sleeping.

"So this is all down to you not being able to sleep?"

Lassie nodded with enthusiasm.

"You wanna bake? Always does the trick for me; little nightcap and I'm out like a light."

My previous experiences "baking" went back to college days. Like most people who say their "baking" went back to "college days," mine extended for a period after too. However, this was years ago, and as Andros got an ornate box out from underneath the coffee table, I felt like a balloon about to burst and was open to anything. From inside the mahogany patterned box, Andros lifted out a bag of what was once referenced as "sweet, sweet cheeba." He opened the bag, picked apart some buds and placed them in a grinder that looked military grade.

"How are we getting guns out of the way here? How does this make any of the states with entrenched gun culture less so?" Andros inquired as he ground his produce.

My Lassie charades informed Andros that guns weren't leaving the hands of a single American; in fact, this plan expected gun owners to take the impetus.

"Right. So, this is something that should work for Cremodats and Irupblecans?" Andros nudged, as he delicately portioned his produce across a king skin on the table. "So where is the money going? All this money raised; seven figures is serious money, Sam."

This part of explaining required more intricate explaining. My effort must have looked like aggressive flash dance by someone who'd just fallen down the stairs. After an exhaustive twenty minutes, Andros understood that the insurers stood to make a profit from shootings, so we needed them on our side. Andros looked puzzled as he handed me the joint.

"But I thought you were trying to stop people shooting one another?"

I took a long drag and sounded like a frog as I said, "I am."

As I was coming up and generally feeling brighter than during the last 12 hours, Andros got out his laptop and showed me the accounts and the array of donations. Most were from the grassroots, small things, $10 to $15 a pop; it was fascinating. I let Andros know I had been round DC and had made my way out south, but I had a little more of the country to travel. Andros said an entire paragraph of speech that I did not hear, and I realized I was high as a kite. I grabbed Andros by the nearest arm and told him to give me his address and wake me at 5. I was on my way to the insurers conference that evening, and Adam said he'd take me there. My last memory was dropping my phone after messaging Adam the address ... then Lassie passed out on the couch.

11

I CAN REMEMBER DREAMING I WAS wriggling on the spot some-where. As I slowly came to, I could feel a hand loosely gripping my shoulder. Then I realized the hand on my shoulder was shak-ing me. Shortly, sound arrived.

"Sam, there's a limousine outside."

Andros wasn't lying. When I sat up to peer through the win-dow, the back door was opened by the driver, and Adam stepped out like a president. The moment he was fully vertical, he did his jacket button up in a single hand movement. The doorbell rang shortly after my sighting of him. Andros mooched his way to the door and opened it. I remember hearing Adam greet him warmly. Andros was marched round the corner into my line of sight with Adam's arm round his shoulder, a gravelly voice filled the air with a musical levity to it.

"It's our accountant! Do I like him, do I like him—"

Adam's faced dropped the moment he looked at me.

"The fuck happened to you? You look more shitty than usual. You have an orgy with 15 homeless guys or something?!?"

Andros being a friend, he did his best to defend me.

"Adam, I swear he was in worse shape when he arrived—"

"Yeah, yeah, let's get this motherfucker in the shower." Adam lurched forward and grappled me off the sofa. His strength was terrifying, he sent me over his shoulder like I was a child.

"I was an amateur wrestler in my youth," he belted out. "I once choked out three gym teachers in a single afternoon."

Andros looked mildly shellshocked as Adam hoisted me through the corridor then dumped me into Andros' shower cubicle.

"You'll thank me later. Believe me," Adam mumbled, pointing the showerhead right at my face. Freezing cold water arrived, my breath left and holy shit, did I wake up. Before I had a chance to process the shock of my body temperature dropping like a bomb, Adam was hauling me out of the cubicle.

"We're strapped for time now, got to get you suit shopping."

I can remember being wrapped in towels, and truly wrapped, like a burrito, lying across the back of the limo. Pins and needles bloomed all over my body as I was soaking wet with freezing cold water while lying on seats heating up by the second. I couldn't even remember saying goodbye to Andros, and I hoped this was as close as I'd ever get to a hostage situation. Adam had positioned me masterfully; I couldn't even move my arms from inside the towels. He sat opposite me giving the occasional smile as he churned off about four calls just on our journey to the menswear place.

To give Adam credit, the suit was a masterpiece. It was an extraordinarily good fit. I have a physique not worthy of any mention ever, but man did I look good in that thing. Standing in the full-length mirror, it was the first time since my late twenties I didn't look like a fat bastard. The color of the pants and jacket was grey, but a subtle unassuming grey; I didn't look like a pump and dump guy or a fool desperate for pussy. My arms have always been pointlessly short, which had perennially made suit shopping a logistical nightmare. However, wearing this thing Adam had found, in the mirror stood one handsome, lean, well-proportioned bastard. Adam appeared in the mirror, standing behind me, and the jackal smiled once again.

"It's a shame about the face ..." He exploded into laughter. I didn't. It was an *actual* shame about the face.

The insurance shareholders' conference was being hosted at a Hilton for the night. By the time the limo pulled up in the parking lot, I'd popped another OxyContin and the limousine's seat warmers had become my friends. As I stepped out of the limo shortly after Adam, there was an exciting air to the place. It was night out and everyone was dressed to the nines; sharp suits and dazzling dresses adorned all. I whispered to Adam that the only thing missing was a red carpet. Adam responded by saying, "We'll get to them later if you're willing to hang around." I asked what he meant, he plainly said, "Publicity. We've got to get *#BelieveAmerica* flying."

The main hall of the hotel we walked into was in full function mode. It had one of the highest ceilings I'd ever seen and half a dozen glittering chandeliers hanging way above us. The entire hall was a landscape of fixed fake smiles and a cacophony of rumbling conversation. At the far end from the entrance, a stage had been constructed with a giant tarpaulin banner hanging above it.

LIVEVA INSURANCE SHAREHOLDER CONFERENCE
"No matter the disaster, we're gonna be rich!"

Adam and I sidled our way across a royal blue carpet oppressed by endless chair and table legs. We were about 40 minutes late to the commencement of the thing; most folks were seated 'round tables sitting upright and looking terrified. It had one of those formality trap vibes, where everyone is too afraid to do anything "wrong," so they are reduced to doing impersonations of themselves at each other. Along the way to try and find our table, Adam was pressing the flesh and introducing me to many people. I don't remember any of their names or what even one of them looked like, yet all the handshakes were a bit too firm for my back's liking.

When we arrived at our table it was like the Adam clone club. Every one of them had jackal-like physical mannerisms; they spent the entire evening on their phones or leaving the table to make a call. This would only be interrupted by a paranoid scowling twitch to look around the room or raising a glass for an impromptu silent toast. It was when a waiter came over and asked for our order that I got the hint. The table had a harmonized chorus response of

"Screwdriver," which sent the waiter on his way. I realized I was sitting at the lobbying/consultancy table. What fun.

The screwdrivers kept arriving at regular intervals, and I'll admit it made the evening go quicker. The only part of the evening I have a clear recollection of was the last of the "opening act" guys. Shortly after the waiter took our order, the lights dimmed somewhat, a spotlight came up on the stage and truly awful stock synth played. A little dude came skipping out to tepid applause; he had a shirt and tie but no jacket and his sleeves rolled up. This was supposed to symbolize he was a "man of action." His opening gambit was warming up the crowd by trying to get us to say things and cheer what he told us to. I did but I was predominantly alone. No one was initially feeling the "hype man."

Maybe the alcohol had arrived at other tables too, but after half an hour of gratuitous flattery and kissing the ass of everyone there, the crowd had picked up. I remember looking up at the little spinner and from the back of the stage, he got out what looked like a ginormous shirt gun. It looked like one of those things bands use to fire shirts into the crowd at gigs. This being an evening for those with money, free t-shirts wouldn't cut it. I don't know who gave the little guy his brief, but the choice of gift for these well-off folks had not been given due consideration. Within two minutes an ambulance had to be called. The little idiot fired a rolled up Persian rug into the audience, a diabolical decision. Furthermore, he did it three times.

Strangely, the medical emergency of the evening seriously gee'd up the crowd. The "hype man's" mission was accomplished. One of the board members took to the stage; he wiped the sweat off his brow with his pocket handkerchief and with a lump in his throat declared, "Ladies and gentlemen, what can you say at a moment like this but *thank God* for insurance." People were instantly on their feet applauding and cheering as the Persian rug "winners" were wheeled off on stretchers. The board member's white in his lacquered side parting could be seen from the other end of the earth and he was cheered on to keep talking. As he began his spiel, a registrar for the evening came to our table asking me for details. Adam leaped across the table screeching like a hyena: *"DON'T SIGN ANYTHING!!!!"*

My head was lolling once again at this point. It wasn't one of my barely-keeping-consciousness lolls; it was more being so relaxed on alcohol and painkillers that posture no longer applied. As I lolled, my vision across and around the room was a barely interrupted haze, yet I managed to spot a strangely familiar face. There was a mildly orange looking male in a suit among pasty males seated at the table. The face resonated; it was Irupblecan House Speaker Jan Blamer. Within minutes, he started moving across the room toward our direction, shaking hands and faux cheek kissing along the way.

Blamer's face burst into warmth upon seeing Adam. Adam returned the warmth by getting to his feet and opening his arms. His head tilted on an angle as he beckoned a hug. He looked like a shit dad from a hokey sitcom. Blamer welcomed the embrace, and the two of them launched into a gravelly voice off. I couldn't make out a word. After Adam had made his way round our table introducing the House Speaker to everyone, Blamer reached into his jacket pockets and threw four packs of cigarettes on the table,

"You oughta try these. The people at the tobacco companies told me they're really good for you."

Blamer vanished into the night, and I was left with side parting from hell up on stage. He was doing his best to be inspirational; it all sounded deranged.

"… 300 companies have gone under, nearly 100 people are facing federal charges and it's been reported over 30,000 have been fired, but ladies and gentlemen, we have 00000.01% GROWTH!"

Most tables in the room levitated into the air with celebratory punching and high fives all round. Even in my haze, I didn't find the trappings of corporate law anything to be doing high fives about and I wanted to move on. Getting out of my chair, I slowly waddled over to Adam. He put a forefinger up to me. I'd been so rude as to interrupt one of his 600 phone calls. After a couple of murmured responses, he placed the phone up against his jacket. "Whaddya want?"

"What are we doing here, man? When are we moving and shaking?"

"I'm organizing that. Go make yourself busy. Go talk to people. We'll be off soon."

So I followed Adam's advice. Most of the tables didn't look like they wanted to be bothered by anyone but the folks standing around at the back in conversation looked more promising. I had the illusive pleasure of talking to four Harvardians back to back. That meant four bipedal turrets of arrogance telling me ferociously about how they went to Harvard, with shit-eating grins for good measure. I stood there as my soul drained down to the floor, probably down a sewer beneath.

To the side of the hall were a couple of vintage-style suited skinny guys in thick-rimmed glasses looking meek and nervous. One had a stretched Milhouse vibe to him, so I approached his visible terror feeling that I couldn't lose. Within a foot of him, his trembling voiced pitch arrived: "Social media is the next and only plateau of investment. Why, you can buy stocks in something valued at $500 million that's generated exactly $0 revenue."

I guess spending a lifetime in front of computer screens kind of cooks your logic. Like a humane pet owner having to put an animal down, I let them know I was there to pitch too. The Milhouse fanned his shirt a bit and blew out his cheeks. He and his perm-haired tech pal looked relieved they didn't have to guarantee anyone's confidence. We bitched a little bit about the evening and what we were doing for the night. They must have been mid-early twenties but were clearly professionally developed. I was staggered that America could produce more and more of these professionally blessed magical munchkins.

I enquired of Silicon Valley. I was intrigued about the place that had shaped the modern world. The Milhouse told me most Google employees only lasted around a year before moving on voluntarily, as the pressure of everyday coding or programming wasn't worth the cost on quality of life. The permed friend nodded. I figured for a moment. I then asked the Milhouse if that wasn't a damning indictment of landing a job for the most famous and wealthy company on the planet. Both tech stick insects stood silently before slowly looking down at the floor adrift. The awkward silence was broken by a large, padded hand slapping on my shoulder.

"We got to get over to Beverly hills, let's go," Adam purred.

I wished Milhouse and the perm well before Adam and I returned to our limousine.

12

S POTLESS STONE PATIO GLIMMERED BEHIND gates that led up to a front porch big enough for a titan to walk through. Two fifteen-foot pillars belonging to a baby Parthenon announced the draw bridge-esque front door inside a porch made entirely of marble. The mansion basked in glowing orange spotlights illuminating the front. Our limousine came to a stop outside the gates and Adam turned to me inside the limo.

"This is a party for awards season."

"But awards season isn't for months."

"Yeah, these people get pretty excited about awards. It's for Tim Della Haklin, you know the one, intense method actor type, he's got a film called *The Bushman* coming up, supposed to be 'his moment.' Just say supportive things, don't tread on anyone's ego and look for established stars."

"Why look for the established stars?"

"'Cus they've earned all their money, they've got all their fame, they finally feel validated and now they want to be remembered for something instead of dressing up and making pretend as a fully grown adult. They're publicity magnets; they're insecure, and eager to please; we could find some useful idiots in here."

The limo entering the driveway was an enjoyable moment. Adam and I stepped up to the front porch in unison. Adam leaned forward and rang the austere, raised front bell. The castle keep, at least a 10-foot door, slowly levered open, and a maître 'd for the evening appeared before us.

"Good evening. May I ask, are you on the guest list?"

"Is Ivan Zlobec-Bolha here?"

The maître d', dressed in all figure-hugging black, paused. I think she was shocked, but her flawlessly peeled and plucked face didn't move at all, so it was quite hard to tell. She ran her hand down her ponytail that nearly reached the floor.

"Er, can I ask why—"

"It's OK, I'll phone him."

Adam got out his phone and started a call while the three of us stood there basking in awkwardness. The maître d' was esthetically flawless, and I felt odd just standing there. I figured I'd introduce myself.

"Hi, I'm Sam."

"That's nice ..."

Ivan was a long-time producer out in Hollywood. He had a flowing paisley shirt on, spectacles in his pocket and skin that had been left out in the California sun for a decade too long. Ivan burst into volcanic laughter at every other sentence. I couldn't tell if this was an immense enjoyment of life or what is clinically known as "manic defense." Adam and he seemed to go way back, and they greeted each other giddily. When I asked Adam how they knew each other, Adam only said he'd "got him out of tough spots a few times." I wish I knew what that meant.

The main foyer we walked into was only semi populated. It was a gorgeous, grandiose hall of even more marble and a dreamlike giant staircase that splayed into two long winding staircases up to a second floor balcony. The industry's biases and hierarchies were visible in an instant. On the ground floor were the crew and background artists and to be frank with you, they looked as happy as they were desperate to be there. Hugging the walls of the ground floor were more interesting folk. They were predominantly male, they all looked various degrees of unwell and were, in fact, teachers. We'd found the screenwriters.

Making our way up a staircase that could have been up to the pearly gates, faces appeared that I recognized more. There was an array of good actors, the dudes you actually like. Not the assholes baying for their name being bigger than the title of the story they're supposed to be in, but the supporting actors. Those actors who are simply good at acting without any bells, whistles and bullshit. There was the curly haired guy with a paunch and a depressed face who could be pathetic or heartbreaking in whatever he was in. I put out my hand when we passed, and he shook it and smiled. I'd just met eternal supporting actor winner Lon D. Miley.

At the doorway of the second floor lounge and spilling into it were all the superheroes, like, all of them. I saw the Norse Gods from space, their names eternally mispronounced; and despite being Nordic, they both sported stiff British accents. There was the Strange one; despite a name like that and a secluded existence, he wasn't on any offenders registers anywhere. Maybe having control of time itself helps with stuff like that. Pretty sure I spotted the insect schoolboy with that disgusting habit of ejaculating out his wrists … all over buildings, people, cars … anything—disgusting. The Guardians of CGI and makeup were also present. The big, angry, green bastard was inside, but he wasn't all that angry, big or green. Having spoken to him, he clearly wasn't a scientist either. The Ant may have been there … I couldn't find him anywhere. Inside the lounge, was the man himself, LED heart, give-a-shit, tin-suit man. A walking wet dream of private enterprise, he'd done well out of the movies; I understood he made $64,000 every time he blinked. The scene was something to behold, but this was Hollywood, and I couldn't help but notice something. Then my mouth ran away again.

"Hey superheroes, where are all the Wakandans?"

Most of the room turned to face me in a slow chilling rotation like gargoyles coming to life. A hand grabbed me by the elbow, and I was suddenly shuffling forward. My first sense on entering the lounge should have been excitement, but it was Adam in my ear.

"Now what the fuck did you have to say that for? *They'll be on SSRI's for 18 months over that!!!*"

Further inside, the second floor lounge was some weird shit. After earning enough money, apparently you no longer must differentiate between couch and bed. An open plan, tile-floored room

was swamped with deranged bed-couch hybrids, and all were lit-
tered with stars. Surrounded by dazzled up and comers was Trevor
Night Tulips, the gangly English-Irish man who'd won so many
Academy Awards some actors hit a black depression upon sight of
him. He'd been through recent allegations he had been using a time
machine to prepare for roles. Luckily for his fellow actors, Trevor
Night Tulips only made a film every blue moon or eclipse. Between
roles, he did perfectly normal things, like eat live goldfish, howl at
traffic or pluck hedgehogs.

Adam and I were introduced to the circles and little hubs of
chatting actors by Ivan. While a lot of their faces appeared to have
great difficulty moving, they could snap into a smile in 0.03 seconds. The next couch-bed thing we passed, there was one of the
humanitarian actors. They had a bad-ass past but had since become a modern day biblical patriarch with a Noah's ark of children.
Unlike biblical patriarchs, she was worth several million and looked
outstanding in a dress. There was a scrunched up, desperate agent
on the couch talking to her. The agent assured her he'd landed career-making parts to men every month and a career-making part to
a woman once every decade. She didn't look so impressed with that.

Finally, making a clearing where we could see Tim Della
Haklin, he was already surrounded by suits. Adam and I slowly
shuffled our way towards the couch where Tim was talking shop
to the producers. Ivan whispered in between me and Adam, "Isn't
Tim some kind of genius?" Adam nodded furiously, I less so. For
the record, I liked Della Haklin. He got involved in all the shit you
loved about actors: fake accents, wigs, prosthetics, funny walks, epic
crying scenes and, my all-time personal favorite, "shouty acting."
Tim raised an open palm upon sighting Ivan, and the suits got their
cue and slowly drifted from him.

His perfect slender face with masterfully gelled hair beckoned
us on as we moved towards Della Haklin. His movies were some of
my favorites. He was kind of in the mold of the Method dudes back
in the '50s and '70s. Tim was yet to win his Academy Award, but
half the population of internet users had decided him winning one

was a matter of existential importance. I did like Tim Della Haklin, but he had the "method actor" thing of telling you everything he did to prepare for the role in every interview. Within a foot of him, I reminded myself it was all PR and part of the game for the cameras; I never met him in person.

Adam, near vibrating with excitement, put out a hand for shaking.

"Tim. Pleasure to see you once again. How are ya?"

Della Haklin tilted his head and squinted as he slowly placed his hand to meet Adam's.

"Aaaaa-dum?"

"That's right!" Adam chirped, completely unfazed by having not been all that remembered.

"Good to see you too, man. Yeah, I'm good. Great to hear the distribution's got the timing it has. I'm feeling good … bit of relief too. I tell ya, I spent three and a half years down a ravine in outer Patagonia, eating my feces, drinking my urine, even starting families with livestock just to prepare for this role."

I popped another OxyContin and it wasn't for the pain in my back.

As the night continued in balmy, glowing glamor in the hills of LA, the actors weren't that bad. Once enough alcohol had evaporated from their glasses, the air of FOMO and insecurity drained considerably. They had jarring habits of monologuing or performing stories at each other, but to be fair, they were pretty entertaining stories. I'd never had a chance to consider it, but most of their tales of the industry involved blatant forms of humiliation. What was more alarming was that 90% of these tales of humiliation came from men who were all white. I zoned out imagining the bullshit that everyone else in the industry was made to go through. Adam and Ivan's bubbly demeanor had loosened the invisible shackles of the evening, and suddenly the floor was Adam's and mine.

For the first time, I got to see Adam working his craft, and my newly found jackal friend was a talented soul. Half these actors should have taken lessons from Adam; he became a different person right in front of me. His body and voice softened, holding the circle in a dulcet tone. He spoke about me like I had saved an orphanage from a blazing inferno; it was remarkable. Out of seemingly nowhere, Adam was emotionally full with a tight throat and enlarged, serious, wet eyes. In fairness to Adam, he even stopped my mind in its tracks, reminding me why we were doing all this—children *are* being shot dead in schools and a lot of people are being shot beyond.

When it came my turn to speak after a poetic handover from Adam, the room was full of eyes all looking up at me. Amazing, movie-star eyes, and not only the ones that had three decades of surgery surrounding them, all on me. My usual pro forma came along well; the two actresses present reached for the Kleenex. For whatever reason, I took a tangent onto the "AK-forty pooches act" that got some animal activists in the room fuming. That *really* wound them up. They had to be consoled by fellow actors telling them they were "*a worthwhile person worthy of love*," yet it was the Twitter account that hooked them.

The moment the tweets were read out and didn't sound all that bad on the ear, the second floor lounge full of actors found a new lease of life. The periphery of the gathering surrounding us got lighter. Everyone on the edges of the group slinked off. Initially I had a bad feeling we were losing them, but I could see they were all getting their phones out. We weren't losing them; they were phoning their agents and publicists to see if they could be a part of this. The more I laid out the tenants of "SLSGs Believe America" the more they loved it; bipartisan, for morality, for children, in a movement for everyone, all across the country. Della Haklin and a couple others had hash tagged *BelieveAmerica* before it was even time for us to leave.

It was 1 am when Adam and I drunkenly slumped back into our limo. Howling in delight the moment the door closed, Adam practically leapt on me in a flying hug. His big, padded, fluffy hands ruffled my hair and he crawled across the limo floor to the drinks cabinet. Pouring a tall whisky he purred, "That was a modern day masterpiece. They gobbled it up! They goddamn gobbled!!!"

"It was 80-90 percent you, Adam, you got the 'people thing', you can hold a room. It's been a pleasure working with you," I declared as I raised my tumbler of whisky. Adam met it with his, and the limo pulled out of the driveway. Letting out a belch that dented the window between us and the driver, Adam pulled out his cell phone.

"FANTASTIC! The account has hit a million over Tim GOD DAMN DELLA HAKLIN! We're flying Sam! We're GODDAMN FLYING! This thing's gonna be 'UGE!!" Adam downed his whisky and demanded the limo driver play AC/DC. The limo driver said he didn't have AC/DC. Adam then demanded the limo driver "take us somewhere with AC/DC." At this point, between his swaying slur and ludicrous demands, it dawned on me Adam was quite drunk. I was barely a picture of sobriety, and I couldn't get comfortable in the limo after Adam's flying bear hug, so I popped another OxyContin to take care of that.

As the limo slowly trawled its way through the gated communities of these notorious West Coast hills, Adam pointed to all the different mansions and told me who lived there. Adam was full of stories of whom he'd met at one time or another. Whenever the person was a household name, his teeth became visible and his eyes went wide: full jackal. The tall and sprawling mansions and their gates all looked increasingly out of focus. I was close to passing out when I remembered—I wasn't even in Cali to see the movie stars.

"Adam, what … what about the insurance shareholders and all them? What happened?"

"Oh, well that's probably a few rounds in as we speak."

"What?"

"They will be receiving 'gifts' for participating and giving us their support."

"What? What gifts? I don't understand."

"In order for us to have the support and backing of insurance boardrooms they have been given 'gifts' as a 'thank you', out of 'good faith', on this night."

"… the fuck's a 'gift'?"

"Company."

It landed like a brick.

"HOOKERS?!?"

"I prefer escorts or courtesans."

"FUCK-ING COURTESANS???"

"Well, literally, yes."

"Jesus fu … Adam, *why are we buying hookers for people??!?!*"

"We're not buying, it's all coming out of the PAC."

"DEAR GOD, HOW MUCH???"

"'Bout 60 to 80 thousand."

"Sixty to eighty thousand *on hookers*! FOR A NIGHT?? *ARE THEY TRYING TO JIZZ THE PLANET OFF ITS AXIS???*"

"Oh, I've done all this before," Adam said, like we were standing in line at *Subway* …

13

THE CEILING WAS A FADED dull white covered in cobwebs and didn't look all that dry. I shuffled just a little and my back let out a seismic crack letting me know I probably shouldn't move. As I tried to sit up my hands and skin got stuck to the spot they were on. Leather, the sticky nasty of leather when you've been unfortunate enough to thoroughly sweat on it. I was sticky and gross and realized I was on Andros' couch. When I managed to get myself to sitting, Andros was perched on the coffee table with a mug in his hand.

"Thank you for putting me up." My voice had a croak in it that belonged to no living being.

"I wouldn't say I had a choice Sam," Andros said, pressing a thumb rhythmically into his palm. He looked despondent.

"How bad?" I asked, not really wanting to know.

"Well, I need a new shower."

"Oh shit, what happened?"

"Adam happened. Having managed to wake all my neighbors while busting my speakers with a full volume AC/DC tribute, he got inspiration to rip my shower cubicle out of the wall declaring, 'This fucker saved us' … um … he then carried out my entire shower cubicle through my hallway—which now needs reflooring—threw the cubicle into the back of the limousine and drove off into the early morning with it."

"I'll cover the shower and the floor, that's fucked up, I'm sorry. What's my hit list looking like?"

"Mainly, you just tried to make sure Adam didn't take the toilet with him. You were very insistent on letting us know, er, what was it? Your back 'doesn't like it' when you shit or something? You then got stuck in a loop yelling at my ceiling fan, 'I didn't embezzle nothing you flying fuck,' then you passed out on the couch claiming your back hurt."

It was a shameful display on reflection. Andros had always been a great friend, and I didn't like hearing the review of our drop-in. I popped an OxyContin so I could stand and placed a hand out to Andros.

"I said I'd buy you a beer next time I'm in Cali."

Andros' period-piece car wasn't the worse thing to be driven in when hungover. Cruising along the boulevard, looking along the lawns, I had forgotten how idyllic a morning in California could be. The thick crisp of the air and the glow of warm light when the rays of sun flooded the grass. Cali felt flat and expansive and stoned and a world unto itself. I loved the warmth, I loved that everyone looked a million dollars irrespective of the means. Maybe Magda was right, maybe I only needed a getaway in the sun.

The Datsun clunked as we pulled up next to a bar along a strip of cheap vendors. Andros said this was his favorite. The décor outside was loud, but the open door revealed that inside was cozy and secluded. I had my OxyContin blur on and was pretty sure I shouldn't be drinking, but a beer with Andros was the least I could do. My pocket vibrated and I got out my phone. Adam, with a declaration of love:

THIS PACIAS THING IS ANOTHER MASTER-STROKE FROM THE MAESTRO. WAY TO BRING IN A SWATHE OF THE WORKING CLASS DEMOGRAPHIC. GOD BLESS. A

Working class demographic? I checked the Twitter account and there was a drunken post solely stating,

PACIAS. #SLSG #BelieveAmerica

It had cracked 20,000 re-tweets, so I was naturally fascinated. As we entered the bar, I scrolled through all the accounts that had retweeted it, and the account holders were overwhelmingly Hispanic. Furthermore, they all appeared to be working in forms of manual labor. As Andros and I took a stool at the bar, I still had no idea what PACIAS meant. According to Google, it was Spanish for "graze." When I took my first sip of beer, I remembered why I'd posted it. I wasn't writing Spanish; it was a drunken attempt to acronym "pop a cap in an ass." No more early morning tweets for me …

After a little bit of pushing, I managed to convince Andros I should very much be paying for and getting the beers. The bar surface was more clean than sticky, given the hour of the day. There was only one old boy sitting in a booth by himself towards the back of the bar. When our beers arrived, Andros was looking over at the hunched little old timer, by himself, with his paper. I lifted the glass to my mouth and a sweet swig of the beer hit my tongue. A cool flume of liquid traveled down my gullet and within seconds, the edge of a hangover was relieved.

"I thought your Mom told you not to stare." I nudged Andros, trying to bring back his attention.

"Look at him. You get there is no guarantee either of us won't end up like that."

"Ah Jesus, if this is your way of bringing the mood down thanks to last night, I'd prefer you were just angry at me. You can let me have it, man, we didn't respect your place or yourself."

"Forget the place, it's a dive anyway, although I prefer having a shower to not having one. I'm serious man … look at him. When was the last time you had someone? Don't you ever get the feeling that … maybe this is it? Maybe we're unappealing, inoffensive and then … you don't repel anyone, there's really not all that much to you. So nobody sees you. Then you end up old and alone in bars reading papers … till you die."

I took a healthy gulp of my beer. I couldn't contend existential bleakness and a hangover at the same time. It had to be one or the other.

"You'll find someone, dude. You're a musician, for Christ sake, I don't even know if this is your battle."

"Huh?"

"You're a musician. Swap the drunken hookups for phone numbers and you might get someone to stay with you sometime."

"Plenty of ladies wanna do coke and have a night with a gigging saxophonist, not many want to live in a house with one."

"Well shit, man, I'm not Dr. Phil."

"Alright, alright. What about you then?"

"Eugh. I … when those things happened, they always came to me … if they were good. I don't go out much."

"Neither do I, nor do most people I know, it's expensive."

"What happened to people, man?"

"They broke the unions, devalued real wages, shoved adverts down everybody's throats while drowning them in harsh news. We stay home with our floor space and endless things. We've retreated."

We got about halfway down our beers. The conversation moved on freely. For all the pangs of loneliness, Andros was happy in his life. He showed me photos of the gigs and the several household name musicians he'd bumped into along the way. Whether it was the beer or moving on from our single-guy-moping, Andros seemed to like my thesis on the situation; maybe a little bit of loneliness along the way was the tax for getting to do the job you love.

My glass appeared to have beer evaporating from it; I suspected that I was responsible. There was a moment of quiet between us. What I said to Andros was true and wasn't true. Nobody I'd been close to really got to know me. Though I'd been actively searching less and less. I knew though and it—

"Hey, space cadet, where'd you go?"

"Sorry. I'll get us another one."

"Get you another one, I'm driving—then we're going shower shopping."

The moment the beer was placed in front of me, we were back to talking shop. Andros was curious while holding an air of total insecurity in what had happened so far. He told me outright that

Adam was an "embodiment of weird," but he was keen to see where it was all going. I told Andros I wasn't sure, but I was certainly trying to build a "coalition of the willing." I gave him the details of all those informed so far. He was happy to hear every tale, from the DC liberals to the Sooner Militia and most recently, apparently, Latin American manual laborers.

Andros laughed a little. "Look, you've got money and an ever-growing internet presence on your side. This is all good. But when it comes to people … I mean come on …"

"Wha?"

"You've mainly spoken to various degrees of upset or frightened white people … and in majority, men. America has a whole lot more to it than that, pal. Go speak to everyone you can, everyone not like you, see what they make of this. See what comes from it. Save Lives, Save Guns has made an amazing start. Imagine where it could go."

The hangover was dissipating along with my mood rising. Andros was right. This was still early days, and so many Americans were yet to have their say and input. I couldn't wait. The sun grazed across the bar floor through the open door, revealing a sidewalk drenched in light. My hand grabbed my beer and I put it away.

"Alright, let's go buy you a shower."

"And a new floor."

"Yeah, shit."

We turned off our stools and ambled our way to the door. I could barely open my eyes with all the sunlight as Andros' car keys jingled in his hands as we left.

"Sam. Is your back just like that now?"

14

THE WEIGHT OF THE MOVEMENT and the PAC and its possibilities accompanied dense insomnia. Soon back in DC, the state of the schools only fueled my charge that our children could be taken better care of. Work provided plenty of odd looks in relation to my back. I tried sitting in different directions and angles, but I was some kind of slanted idiot. The OxyContin surged through my veins; I wasn't in physical pain over my back, but constricted and moving oddly. It was fall in DC. My time between sitting in the basement bunker was listless, trying to find the next place to be.

Marching along the Potomac, an infrequent, fierce breeze kept gunning at me. The still of the rich, dark blue water seemed to rest my unease walking. My back felt equivalent to a mouth numbed from an intrusive dental appointment. No pain but the presence of where pain should be residing made itself apparent with every step. I thought about making a trip into the American History Museum but I reneged. Figured all I'd find in there was a long line of wars with everybody. The one time we ran out of people to declare war on, we just started kicking the shit out of each other …

Sun infrequently peered from behind the clouds on a solidly overcast day, and I soon found myself at the memorials. The scale of it all hit me: sure, we had been to war with everybody at least once and that included ourselves … and that meant a lot of people had died in the name of this country.

The Korean War memorial looked as alive as I remembered from childhood. These cloaked figures, everyone so distinct, rifle in hand, making their way through terrain unknown. Shadows fell from their helmets when the sun would reappear in cameo. There was genius in this design, they felt real to me. I stood a while confronted by the faces rendered in the marble in memorial of WWII. Every face did not fit today. These were different faces, from different times, shining through from only an artist's impression in some stone tablet somewhere. Yet how fresh they were, how wide-eyed, how unblinking. All the faces showed youth, men, boys, women, girls, workers, soldiers; all in contrast yet all together. I stood looking for a good ten minutes; we don't have this unity anymore, and I didn't wanna leave.

The soothing splash of water from fountains of the WWII plinths echoed around me. My father was clear to tell me the details of World War II that the history books wouldn't. While in his eyes he could never forgive FDR for (in his words) "manipulating" the US into WWII, he also said, "Every last son of a bitch alive ought to be grateful that he did." He would get so animated telling me these stories on car journeys as a kid. Animated to a point where my Mom would butt in to sedate his energy. Eyes bulging, hands aloft in gesticulation (off the steering wheel much to my mother's chagrin) trying to convey to me that no matter how much he said, he was "only throwing words at the unimaginable." At the Atlantic Theatre tribute, as a little more sun peeped out and kissed the marble before me, my eyes met words I hadn't seen since I was 10 or 12 years old. Hurtgen Forest.

This was where Grandpa Johnson lost his left leg and had his arms so scarred that, to his deathbed, he would rarely allow himself to be seen in short-sleeve shirts. This was a place that Papa Johnson told me, "nightmares would hide from." Then I went looking for myself when I was just a little older, and what the words in the books told, made my father's tales look dampened down in comparison. "The Killing Fields," the books called it. Seven thousand dead in four weeks. A body per yard. "The Meat Factory," the books called it. Barbed wire to mangle you. Artillery-shelled treetops raining shards of hot metal and wood to slice flesh below. Falling trees to crush anything beneath. Unending machine gun fire to tear humans in half. "The Green Hell," the books called it. Hysterical yelling of, "No more killing, no more killing." Night time yelps of, "Shoot me, shoot me." Desertion rates astronomically high. Deafening nonstop noise for weeks on end. Come darkness, a forest floor freezing over and taking many a human with it. Medic was only a word; utterly overwhelmed and rendered useless. Yeah. My Grandad survived that.

I began to feel a little full and took myself away from the WWII stuff. The way Dad told it, Hurtgen might as well be where the Johnson legacy begins. Grandpa came back so deathly serious that his son would observe, "He wouldn't have smiled for a thousand orgasms." Yet my father also explained, he came back with a furious conviction that war on that scale could never, ever be repeated by any society under any conditions. That there was not a reason in hell, heaven, or on earth to go anywhere near that level of destruction again. Grandpa's poor health meant he only saw the early years of 'Nam but his conviction was soon supplanted to his son. Since about his twelfth birthday, my father told me Grandpa had him working his elocution and thinking in ideals; he guided his son towards politics whether he liked it or not. So Papa Johnson went in, to reach across the aisle, to do the right thing, to find compromise and middle ground. Before I walked away from the WWII stuff entirely, the Marshall quote caught my eye, "… *a symbol of freedom on one hand and of overwhelming force on the other.*" Well, maybe middle ground has never been our thing …

Making my way towards the monument, surrounded by the array of memorials, slivers of sun glimmered off the Tidal Basin. I scanned all around me and I had no doubt DC could be a beautiful, and stirring location … shame about a lot of its employees. I popped an OxyContin as my back began aching after too much walking for a given day. As a breezy, liquid feeling of ease began to arrive, I stared at the nearest edge of the Basin. Jefferson, Roosevelt,

King, Lincoln—Andros was right. It was all about men. If not all, then near all. What the hell had it got us? Every tribute to a guy here was either a eulogy or a war memorial ... Andros was right. I needed to talk to women.

It was only approaching midday, I could make a flight if I was smart. The aged and faded maroon on the walls, the metal making up every surface of the basement, the thick muggy air; I didn't want to go back to work. However, it crossed my mind walking through Constitution Gardens that my work attendance had to be getting noticed. The day was a fair one, and the Mall was always something when taken time to be appreciated, but disquiet crept through my mind. I got out my phone and made a call to Natalie.

"Hey," I said, sounding sadder to my ear than I considered myself to be.

"Sam! How are you? You coming into today or ..."

"Er, I gotta get someplace."

"For research?"

"Yeah."

"Sam, you get we're allowed to go whenever, but you've got to log and account for any expenditure that's going to come out of outgoings."

"Yeah, yeah, of course."

"You haven't kept one receipt, have you?"

"Look, I've been busy."

"If this is about your back, you can say, it's not ..."

Natalie's voice trailed off. It was weird, I had not considered my back the perfect alibi to essentially do whatever the fuck ever I liked. Furthermore, I couldn't tell if Natalie was being genuine in raising the issue of my back or trying to slip me an excuse. I nodded, looking out over the waters of the gardens.

"Yeah ... Magda always suggested rest."

"Where are you off to?"

"Boston."

"Bahs-ten," came a horrendous impression on cue.

"Hey. Was it you that said something about volunteer programs out there?"

"I … don't know? Oh. You mean REACH."

"Is that what you were talking about the other day?"

"Yeah, yeah. REACH. The program for domestic violence survivors out in Mass."

"Gotcha. Well, catch ya when I'm back."

"Don't mind me, Peter Pan."

Possession mode kicked in once again; my legs marched me towards the nearest lane of traffic. Upon approach, I had an arm in the air. I got in a cab to Reagan, to fly me out to Logan and on my journey. A tweet reflected the gendered terrain the movement was heading towards:

America's not to be run like a business, as our forefathers would, it's to be run like a home, as the women who raised and made us would.
#MAKEAMERICASAFEAGAIN #BELIEVEAMERICA

15

THE POSITIVE SIDE OF BOLTING to Boston was the cheap and short flight. I didn't take any chances with my back. I spent 70% of the flight on my feet, making irregular trips to the bathroom to pop another OxyContin from a sly jacket lining stash. The place I had an address to was over in Brookline, not a far trip from Logan Airport. The idea was a quick turnaround and getting back to DC that very night. It was less than a ninety-minute flight, and I was sure this work for the movement would only leave me more inspired. I got in a taxi outside arrivals and gave the cabbie the address. Soon we were coursing through the Callan tunnel and I was on my way.

I got a strange soothing out of being in Boston. It was one of those places that held pleasant childhood memories. Dad had a fair amount of business in Massachusetts during his eternal career. So, with his increasing familiarity of it, across my childhood and in fairness, well into my teenage years, we'd take family trips to the harbor. My mom was convinced he was tagging us along purely to get in personal pilgrimages to the crab places. While this may have been true, bringing us along soon made Mom and me converts; so, the politician won over his constituents. The sun was usually blazing. I think we always went in June or July, hiring a Winnebago for a long weekend. As a kid I loved looping my way around the New England Aquarium; I have only memories of pure fascination of the giant circular tank at the center of the place. This, when not leisurely taking in the rays usually with Dad playing tour guide much to Mom's irritation. Then we'd finish the day out with a crab dinner, as a family, as the sun set across the harbor.

As I stepped out the cab, the address from the online post was faced on the side of the stoop before me. This wasn't for the program that Natalie had tipped me off to but for a class I'd found on message boards talking about REACH. A couple of steps down and I was at a basement-level door. I could hear murmuring and movement before the door flung back with certainty, and a clear face with brown hair tied back peered through the gap.

"Hello …" the face said in uncertainty with eyebrows raised for added effect.

"Hi, my name's Sam. I'm here to speak to Sharon Argeton."

"Speaking," she said in a still bewildered tone. "Have we met?" The bewildered voice then accompanied with a furrowed brow.

"We haven't, I work for a think tank in DC. We're working on gun violence prevention and, um, you know, as a leader on women's issues, I was hoping to pick your brain."

Sharon tilted her head and leaned against the wall. "Do gooder, are we?" she asked with a cheeky smirk.

"I, uh, if you like—"

"Look, Sam, I'm as frustrated on guns as the next person but you come back another time—"

"Just 15 to 20 minutes, I flew out here to talk to you."

Her face was a picture of unimpressed. Sharon opened the door wide and gestured me in on the spot. "You boys always have to swoop in and play the hero, don't you?" was the audible mumble that accompanied my entrance. We shuffled through into a dimly lit hallway adorned with frames filled with family photographs. The photos themselves were *American Gothic* looking stuff from the Argeton family.

We entered a small, drab-green carpeted room with handed-down furniture and a clear over-population of people. Sitting on the couch adorned with a white handmade quilt blanket were three women. They looked somewhat perplexed by my presence.

The green carpet, a relic from the years of postwar homemaking, was covered in gym mats. There was another woman with stark red hair in slacks stacking the mats away. The tone of Sharon's introduction suggested I was an individual with little bladder control and no awareness of that fact.

"Heyyyyy everyone, this is Saaaaam."

One of the women on the couch piped up. "Are you here to be our target practice?" to a chorus of warm chuckles.

"I hope not," I said to a cacophony of approving lady sounds.

"Sam has joined us from DC to talk about gun violence prevention," Sharon said, taking charge of the proceedings.

"This isn't the worst place to start," one of the women on the couch said.

They were finishing up and on their way out of Sharon's place, but Cathy, Erin, Maggie and Rhonda gave me the brief. They'd been running self-defense classes for women in Boston for the last few years. Programs like REACH in Mass at points even had crossover. Experiences of domestic violence were predominantly treated in terms of safeguarding and protecting victims of long-term trauma. However, many victims and those close to victims found a degree of security and sense of empowerment in self-defense training. Unloaded stun guns, empty mace canisters and laminated printouts of different breakaway methods were being packed away along with the mats. The scene before me looked like training to protect people from a breakout of feral animals—no, just men. They inquired about my social life, my love life and had nothing to say in the face of me having nothing to say. Maggie's full bob of tied back curly hair turned at the door as she started making her way out. A knowing look met my eyes as she straightened up her denim jacket.

"I meant what I said. It's close to like a million women who've been shot or shot at by an intimate partner in the States."

"And its closer to five million who've been *threatened* by a partner with a gun," Sharon said.

Maggie's fingernails, a cool turquoise, rhythmically tapped the door frame before she turned to leave. "Good place to start, good luck," she called through from the hallway.

I found myself settled into an armchair no longer in production and therein of quite good quality. This ergonomic friendliness didn't do much for the back, so I picked myself an OxyContin from the stash in my jacket pocket as Sharon came through with our coffees.

"Whatcha got there?"

"For my back," I said, slurping the pill down with a fine coffee made as milky as requested.

"That's an *injury?!?*" Sharon yelped, taking in my silhouette.

"Oh you don't know the half of it."

Sharon wrapped her lips round her teeth and nodded: the response of one who doesn't know how to respond. My OxyContin blur kicked in and this usually made flowing sentences come easier. Then we soon got to the point I'd arrived for: to listen.

"Sam, I'm glad that you're here for the reasons you say you are but … this is … difficult. Hard to know whether to be deflated or infuriated … and you know neither will help. Most these mass shootings are done by guys with histories of domestic violence, so at least one woman's suffered long before a trigger's pulled. Women *are* leading on guns, they have been for a while. They have been calling on us since Columbine. There was a Million Mom March, not that anybody remembers. We've had amazing work from Judy Byron in Seattle, or er … the 'lock it up' program over in Broward county—Gabby Cliffords for crying out loud. You've seen the polling, right? We're always like 15-20% ahead of men in voting in favor of this stuff, from like the '90s till now. Women *are* leading on guns, it's whether people have the stomach to listen to a woman or not."

Sharon picked her coffee back up from the table in front of her, sipped delicately then said in a near defeated monotone:

"They wanna arm teachers … some people. Well, most teachers are women and most women don't own guns." She shrugged. "Always the last voices considered."

Sharon looked at me with her clear blue eyes and lips angrily pursed.

"I go back to what I said to start. We have girls coming in here talking about getting guns. I get the logic; one in three are raped, it's rarely ever us doing the shooting and we're so very easily on the receiving end … but it's the sins of a man's world. Statistically guns in DV households don't make the abused any safer and, and even if it did, what good does arming a woman in defense of an abuser do for her only to face a courtroom conditioned to see her suspiciously? Maybe women should have more guns, maybe that would stand to protect them, but in this world, it'll only betray them."

She perked up with a degree of disgust in her demeanor.

"So with those beautiful nuggets lined up … what have you got for me, Sam? What are the proposals you're talking about?"

Her question hit me like an anvil. Thanks to the 'Contin I didn't feel anything, utterly numbed out. What did I have? What did I have for women? Nothing. I had to cover my tracks and I could feel my face had turned a certain hue of warm red in embarrassment. My hands started to have pins and needles as I wrote down the think tank details for her. I couldn't pitch, I was too embarrassed. I told Sharon (or "Sharon The Great" as I mentally noted her) I'd follow up, with no intention of doing so. As I made myself out of Sharon's that evening, then on to Fenway Park to slump around sports bars in utter male pity over light beer and pain killers, the thought struck me … how many people even think of this thing from a woman's angle? How many people even consider the domestic violence crossover here? Highlights of NHL blasted from the sound systems and the screens around me all in a loud neon glow. In an inebriated state, a tweet was found that magically made sense the next morning.

Thoughts and prayers is an out of office reply, time to show up, turn up, time to do the work.
#BelieveAmerica #SLSG

16

I WOKE UP IN WAMPATUCK STATE Park with a magnificent stag eyeballing me from about forty feet away. It felt like *The Deer Hunter* but I was the deer and he was the De Niro with a gun. My head pounded royally and the full freshness of the forest air felt an affront. I had no belongings but the clothes I had on me and I was flat on my back. My first compulsion was to slump to my side as I felt like I'd fallen asleep on a log or something. Leaning on my side informed; the uncomfortable gnawing mound I felt was my back. Wampatuck was beautiful even with my eyes half crusted closed. When eyesight returned, I was just off a trail surrounded by endless birches and maples as far as the eye could see.

I propped myself up to sitting and was given nothing but a firm dose of nausea. Aside from a headache that could have split a bison in half, I felt a vibration on my lower ribs and I reached for my jacket pocket. Before the phone reached my ear I half caught a glance at the screen, Adam.

"Hey Kid, how's life treatin' ya? Great night last night."

"Huh? I didn't—"

"Fantastic! Look, remember the Hollywood thing we crashed?"

"Yup."

"We gotta scrap that. No good. Junk."

"OK. Why … exactly?"

"They're two-bit, garbage pail jerk offs whose mothers are two-dollar sows."

"Adam, I find actors as irritating as the next human being but why the heat exactly?"

"They ain't following through, kid."

"Ain't … hang on. Why am I 'kid' suddenly?"

"Easy. Take it easy, kid. This is the worst of the west coast. You get a foot-long line of pearly whites praying to go out to lunch with ya, then the next day they'd just as easily hand you a lawsuit."

"LAWSUIT?"

"Na, na, na, na, na. Theoretical. Keep up. They spoke nice at the time but their managers and talent agencies have all got back. Their agents let me know; it wasn't enough about them. Yada, yada, yada, they find out they are not even going to earn $10 million out of this thing—frankly, they were appalled."

"It's not about them though, it's about preventing gun violence, that's the whole point …"

"Yeah, I hear ya kid but no cameras, crowds, carpets, no gold statues—they couldn't give a shit."

"What happened to 'useful idiots'?"

"Eh, maybe they aren't that useful. Anyway, fuck 'em, some of those guys have such big heads they can't even selfie. They can only halfie."

With a moment to sit up and hear the hum of the wildlife and the rustle of the foliage, this message didn't land so badly. It sounded like the momentum of the thing was stalling.

"Adam, thanks for the call and keeping me in the loop. I'm out in Massachusetts and er … we … I …"

"Spit it out kid."

"Maybe this setback is a sign. It's not such a bad thing, us taking our time here. You know? Working with the policy and the substance instead of the publicity and the symbolism. Actually considering the specifics, whaddya think?"

"I don't deliver people's dreams, Sam. I get them in the mood for dreaming."

"O.K, I get that. I'm just feeling with some ground work now, it might not be the worst time to slow it down anyway."

"Slow it down?? What are you? Spiritually autistic? We're on a roll. The call wasn't to tell you the celebs had pulled out on us ... well they have, but one has stayed with us."

"Oh ..."

"Tim Della Haklin, my friend. Mr. teen heart throb turned method actor extraordinaire. He still wants to fight in our corner. Had a phone call from him personally."

"Adam, I get why this is exciting but I really don't think we have to bother Della Haklin right now. We got bigger things to consider."

"Like what? We got Hollywood's biggest name, we gotta run with this. Tim Della Haklin, bay-bay!"

"Yeah but what's he gonna do, Adam?"

"Guys a 'uge eco warrior, haven't you heard? All the kids love him; drives a Prius made of paper mâché, won't even take a piss in the ocean, fantastic!"

"If you insist ..."

"Yeah, I do. If you followed this stuff, Mr. Politics, you'd know he famously went tiger hugging with the Prime Minister of Turkmenistan much to the internet's acclaim."

"I guess that's kinda sweet."

"Yeah. Till a week later. Till the Prime Minister of Turkmenistan puts it on a giant spit roast and eats the whole thing on a Facebook live stream."

"*JESUS CHRIST!!*"

"Oh man, if he was there; he didn't do shit ..."

"Adam, I still think we should consider slowing this thing down. Look, I gotta go, I don't know where I am, thanks for the call and we gotta arrange a meet up soon. I'm serious, you, me and Andros."

"Sounds good kid, count me on board. Need any sniff? Dab? Toot?"

"Bye, Adam."

I hung up, half aggravated, half relieved it was over. The rich forest green surrounded me and I couldn't see Stag De Niro any-where, so I began to make my move. Following my trail for long enough, I trekked my way back to the park entrance, well, the entrance for the campsite of the park. Ahead was a small pavilion; its pastel blue painted slats and white beams decorated a small office.

Speaking to the lady in the office only deepened my disorientation. To her account, the Winnebago ominously lurching over the edge of a lake 200 yards to our right was in fact mine. I didn't need to worry about the keys, they were still in the graffiti drenched door which was hung wide open. The bumper had a loud Hooters sticker on it and trails of beer cans on string. My eyes searched and looked up only to see the Winnebago appeared to have a fin on the top of it. I asked the lady in disbelief if she could see it and I was met with silence. I turned to look at her. Judy winced and declared in cold deadpan: "Some jackass put a surfboard through your sunlight by the looks of things."

Judy wasn't wrong. I was struck by dread as I slowly approached the Winnie. When I was about 20 yards away, a clatter and awkward bang could be heard from inside. Seconds later, a small brunette woman in a nun's outfit fell down the steps and outside. I stopped on the spot and watched her recover from a substantial face plant. Finally bringing her head up, she looked at me and said, "This isn't Atlantic City," then proceeded to puke everywhere.

A ferocious jet of such intensity it nearly brought her to standing. My approach to the Winnebago went from a straight line to a semi-circle to avoid the projectile vomiting nun. I was within touching distance of the cabin door when the nun had emptied her stomach entirely.

"Stop."

I did so. She coughed a little, then turned to look at me, having turned a beautiful landscape into a Jackson Pollock. There could have been a handsome human being there if, well, if she wasn't covered in vomit and profoundly disgusting at that moment.

"Look … this is an outfit but is the guy duct taped to the chair in there a real Hari Krishna? He looks scared, dude. And like, really old. Like, I'm not sure if he's a Hari Krishna or just a middle aged man in a shawl who'd like to go home."

A whimper emanated from inside the Winnie.

"I JUS WANNA GO HOME …"

I was no longer curious to go inside the Winnebago. The hostage situation could wait on the grounds I still had the upper hand. I looked at Puker Theresa.

"What's your name?"

"Trixy."

"No, what's your real name?"

"Fuck you, asshole, I don't owe you that."

"OK, Trixy. Do you need a ride anywhere?"

"You heading back into town?"

"I dunno. I mean, I gotta get outta here."

"Look, it was wild last night, honey."

"I-I-I literally have no recollection. I have no idea what this is. I have no memory of a Winnebago even. I don't know how any of this has happened."

"You remember me?"

"No. Should I?"

"You don't remember anything?"

"No."

"Remember Adam coming by?"

"Wha?"

"You don't remember that?"

"Adam? Weird guy? Fast talker, whisky voice, odd mammal?"

"Yeah, him. He's not the kinda guy to put something in your drink, is he?"

"WHY YOU SAY THAT?"

"'Cus I think he did …"

Trixy and I tidied up the Winnebago. We talked down a bald middle-aged man who was not a Hari Krishna from hiring legal counsel. It was agreed I was an innocent party and her donation was due from Adam, as according to her memory, he was how we were introduced. She soon made her way over to the pavilion and ordered herself a taxi. We chatted a bit. She was a nice lady. Said her miracle vomiting ability was from a stint of fire breathing in youth. Trixy agreed I could call her "Carny" after that anecdote. It seemed to make her smile. When the cab arrived I reneged on the hug farewell as she stank of bile.

I turned 180 to make my way back to the Winnie but was instead confronted by a seething Judy. This time her eyes were electric and her tiny little finger got right up in my face.

"HOW DARE YOU BRING NUNS HERE FOR THAT KIND OF BEHAVIOR!!!"

My mouth ran away again. "Oh, I got a Hari Krishna in there too …"

The slap left my cheek ringing for the next hour. I had twenty minutes to leave Wampatuck State Park or Judy was calling the park rangers on her radio. I retreated to the Winnebago, my best chance was driving out of there. Judy wasn't fucking around.

17

AFTER ABOUT FIFTEEN MILES OF adapting to driving a big vehicle, I remembered there was a bald guy duct taped to a chair in the back. My memory was cued by his sobbing. For the life of me, I couldn't work out why he didn't pipe up earlier. Looking in the rear-view, the non-Hari Krishna wasn't having the best of times. I asked him why he didn't go before. I just got a full diaphragmed bellow: "YOU'VE DUCT TAPED ME TO A CHAIR AND TIED MY BELT AROUND MY WRISTS!"

The man had a point. I pulled up at the next opportunity. Entering the cabin, he was heinously cussing me every name under the sun through gritted teeth as I took the tape off. As he stood up, I asked him if he would be interested in my program of gun violence prevention. His eyebrows nearly hit the ceiling and I got another full-lunged hair-drier.

"YOU MAKE ME *WANT* TO OWN A GUN!" Not every polling or political action will bring warm results. "Make me wanna own an armory, you *demented shit*."

He hurtled down the steps and sprinted out into the clearing. It's like the old saying goes ... you can't win 'em all. What the shit one does with an unwanted Winnebago, however, was the pressing matter. I had a government employee convinced I'd brought a nun back to a state park for debauchery and an innocent slap head who could call me his captor. I needed to move on. So I did. I started down the highway and was heading North. I figured New England was hardly the worst place on earth to be in terms of gun laws and maybe a Winnebago just needed time to be appreciated.

Come two hours of cruising down the highway, I realized a Winnie is essentially a gutted van with furniture and makeshift plumbing installed and I wanted to get out. "The Winnie" was fundamentally *rancid*. There was a roadside service station just a few miles up the road by the time the cabin-cabin fever had arrived. It was heading into dusk, the sun was setting, and a long drive fading to darkness was hardly inviting. Reaching the service station was a welcome reprieve; I was done sitting, wanted to stretch my legs as I could feel the parasitic discomfort in my back was reappearing.

The parking lot was huge, but I made one hell of a scene swinging in a 36-foot Winnebago. The services provided were truckstop classics: Dunkin Donuts, Sbarro and McDonalds. According to the numbers, there are more firearm retailers than the McD's in this country. Sensing the folks at McDonalds could be staring down the barrel of economic catastrophe, figured I'd buy a couple of burgers off them. As I walked into the mall, it was nearly dark out and the lights of the car park began to turn on one by one.

Stepping inside, the floor tiles beneath were blemished by the endless wear of shoe soles. There was only a one-person-deep queue in the McD's ahead. The ambience of the service station was akin to a cheap mall interior: sterile, perfectly forgettable and designed to be walked through, not stayed in. Potted plants decorated the walkways to the various shops. It didn't take too much of a closer look to see the artifice of the plants. The service station mall was forgettable but the faces about looked like tired souls on long trips.

Sitting down at a restaurant single table and biting into my first patty brought a solid E number hit that briefly energized me. There were only two locations in life that creeped me out, one was airports and one was roadside service stations. Two locations whose entire existence is dependent on them not really being anywhere or being anything in themselves. A principality of transition; you arrive only to leave with not much memory for the place. A wise lady I knew once told me that airports were "netherworlds." Looking round this place was more like "nowhere-world."

I dug into my fries as the burger slid through my insides and my McCrash was about to arrive. I scanned around to make sure I wasn't witnessed so I could pop an OxyContin and slurp it down with Coke. An abandoned food tray was opposite me with an empty fries carton and a couple of strewn burger wrappers. Under the tray was a folded-up newspaper. Rubbing the grease off my fingers onto a paper napkin, I reached over and slid it out from underneath the abandoned tray. I flicked through the customary doom and gloom, till a beautiful Black face looked up at me in photograph.

The headline took me aback. It near froze me. She was transgender. The article was covering a transgender murder. The warm, smiling face belonged to someone who had already been through an ordeal being them … then they were shot. The article spoke of this being one of several cases across states throughout the year. My fingers lost their junk food cramming impetus and parked lifelessly in my box of fries. My eyes looked down at the transwoman looking back up at me. The transwomen, of course, I had to speak to the transgender community. Andros was once again right. I got out my phone, took a wander and I was soon through to him.

"Yo."

"Hey, Sam. How's it going?"

"Well, I'm in New England-ish …"

"How's that working for ya?"

"Look … I think … I mean, I'm looking at all kinds of stuff here and um … you know, maybe this thing has got enough momentum as it is …"

"OK … this is the first time I've heard any kind of uncertainty out of you. Everything OK?"

"Yeah man. I … Andros, I'm, I'm looking at what we've got here and … I don't know what this policy does for women."

"Is it designed in spite of them?"

"Na, no, not at all."

"Look, we got so many people excited here and there's just so much money coming in. I'm sure if your plan gets less fellas firing guns about and at each other, the gals are gonna be happy too, right?"

"That's what I used to think ... now I'm not so sure."

My eyes met the eyes in the paper once more.

"Andros, can you look something up for me?"

"Shoot."

"What's the biggest transgender community in the US?"

"You mean where?"

"Yeah, yeah."

"Err ... hold a sec ... OK, your current hub, DC."

"Ow, to hell with DC. Gimme a state, gimme an actual place."

"Second ... second largest transgender population in the US is in ... Vermont."

"No shit."

"Yes shit."

I hung up. I grabbed the last bite of burger and made my way towards the entrance doors. I could not have been more than a couple of hours from VT. As I strolled through the parking lot, the darkness of night was no longer intimidating. I had a destination. I Hoisted myself up into the cab of the Winnie; the back was settled with 'Contin and I wasn't too blurred out to drive. My fingers negotiated with my cell phone till I'd typed in my destination:

PRIDE CENTER, BURLINGTON, VT

The Boss came on the ancient tape player radio. I pumped it up full. My arms turned a comedy size wheel out of the parking lot and I was on my way. Though around that time, the mere thought of publicity had been blood curdling, I was on a high. My mouth ran away again in the form of a tweet spilling out of me.

Only in a safer America, will all rights matter, count and be emboldened.
#SaveLivesSaveGuns #BA

18

COMING OFF THE I-93 IT was night and the Winnebago crossed the threshold to Vermont. Ahead of me in the darkness was the University campus lit up in a pleasing glow. My initial idea had been to drop the Winnie off with a homeless guy as an altruistic "good act" for the day. Then I remembered the toilet was blocked thanks to the tail end of my McCrash and I was fearful of unwanted consequences. One daydream on a carless stretch of long highway, my mind played out the entire thing. I'd be sitting in a bar in Vermont enjoying a cold beer, charismatically waxing lyrical on guns with enticed locals, when a dude would burst in and yelp: "Some crazed homeless guy just drove a Winnebago into Lake Champlain! There's a trail of shit all over Main Street, *you gotta see this!*"

Reality had left me with undergraduate students on a campus late at night. I pulled up off Main Street and popped an OxyContin to give me a floaty blur for encountering new people. There were a couple of millennial-looking students slouching and vaping along, so I tooted the horn and got their attention. Kyle and Marcus made their way up to the cabin as I stepped out and down. After a brief chat and a generous couple of tokes off the joint they were passing between them, on the grounds I could crash on their couch for the night, Kyle and Marcus agreed they would take the Winnebago. The Pride Center would have been on the verge of closing by the time I got there.

After a careful slalom around campus guard routes, I was shuffled back to Kyle and Marcus' place. A firm must of cheap body spray, energy drinks and bong permeated the air as I entered. Lowering myself onto a couch Kyle needn't have told me was his Mom's, it smelled and looked like a boys' place. Minimum upkeep, stuff on top of stuff, food hygiene an elusive priority and a *Taxi Driver* poster on the wall. Despite the inability to wash things or potentially their bodies, the boys had got hold of a 62-inch 8K HD cinema taking up most the wall in front of me. Marcus slumped into the beaten thrift shop armchair in the corner. He picked up a remote, pressed a button and turned on the beast; it was like going into lightspeed.

MSNBC blurred me deeper into the couch; one of those eight-way talking-head screaming matches that was completely indecipherable. I was in the halls of a northeastern university campus, they were young middle class white dudes, "left leaning" wasn't a surprise. After 20 minutes and couple of hits on what I hoped was a bong, the screaming heads were yelling about the Cremodat Party's priorities for the upcoming mid-term elections. Interlaced with the screaming heads were various snippets and facts about Cremodat candidates nationwide. Kyle handed me a glass of cranberry juice (it was all they had), and I started tuning into the snippets instead of the screaming.

The first Cremodat was a state senator seeking re-election called Do Goodly. Ser Do of House Goodly, if you will. Do Goodly came from humble beginnings. Do Goodly had poor and ill relatives. Do Goodly was a wayward kid in youth. Do Goodly went off to study law. Do Goodly then worked in civil rights law. Do Goodly wore an expensive watch. Do Goodly believed in family values. Do Goodly wanted children raised in an America that Do Goodly was proud of. Do Goodly was voted into office to the approval of middle aged women in his district. Do Goodly helped small business owners and community centers all over his district. Do Goodly had whitened teeth and rolled up sleeves. Do Goodly could not stop smiling. Do Goodly stood up on a table to talk to a crowd and looked like he hadn't been told it wasn't that time of the night yet …

Kyle chimed in, "That's our boy."

"You like him?" I asked.

"Oh you should see what the Irupblecans have served up …"

Marcus handed a joint and an iPad over my shoulder and I watched a monstrous dank corner of the internet unfold. In a cramped bar, a 1930s side parting on top of a corporate suit from the same era snarled at the crowd in the YouTube clip. A five-minute puffed-up soliloquy through a routinely coughing crowd about showing faith in the public. Which by the policy suggestions meant investing absolutely nothing in them. He started getting agitated and mumbled something about "floods of them coming over." He cried a little, then won sympathy by saying he loved his wife (his sixth), and I turned off the clip. Do Goodly may have been a 10x8 picture perfect prick, but I got where Kyle was coming from.

Marcus let me know he had lectures in the morning so was heading to his bedroom. I once again thanked him for letting me stay, he just called me "Winnebago Man" and slunk out of the front room on a plume of chuckles. Back on the screen were more Cremodat candidates. Rolled up sleeves for Syracuse. Top button undone and loosened tie for Delaware. Standing on a table in Scranton. A fair few civil and welfare rights lawyers across the East and West coasts. Hell, not one of these people had an upbringing without poverty or tragedy. It was half an hour later, the bong proved completely unnecessary; all saying the same shit and all faces blurring into one … *they were all Do Goodlys.*

Kyle showed me what a "gravity bong" is. I hadn't known a gravity bong before meeting this young man. It's my understanding (memory is hazy on the details) that one needs about a two-liter bottle, that needs cutting in half, ideally a third-two thirds ratio. The "gravity" of the bong is that the upper part is inserted into the lower filled with water, and the pressure of the inhale draws the gravity and the air making the overall bong smaller. Kyle was soon gazing at the ceiling like he had been told nuclear apocalypse was imminent. I, on the other hand, had made the illusively intelligent choice to *listen* to the Do Goodlys: healthcare, infrastructure, social justice, taking on big pharma, childcare. I could hear soundbites left, right and center on all things, all things … but guns.

"Ah, fuck 'em," I announced unapologetically.

"That bad eh?" Kyle murmured.

"What they gotta say about guns, dude?"

"Cremodats are the only people who are gonna do anything on guns."

"That's what they say, isn't it?"

"They got assault weapons ban on the books, right?"

"That ended 10 years ago and it doesn't appear to have done much while it was in play …"

"Would you rather leave it in the hands of the Irupblecans?"

"No, no, no. Don't try that shit with me. They're doin' their bit. They're on another side to that debate. They are doing their side of the arrangement. I'm talking about the people who've said they will pass laws to protect people from gun violence, they aren't doing their part, they're just saying shit."

"At least there's somebody saying it, man," Kyle said in an almost defeated tone.

"No."

There was a silence between us. I could feel the mood in the room had changed. There was something charged, an air of hostility filled the atmosphere. Then my mouth ran away again.

"Na, that's bullshit, man. That's a script somebody fed you. That's an opinion someone else would like you to take on for their spiritual convenience. We're talking about children and civilians being maimed and killed here, and all we have is a bunch of champagne socialists with a bucket of sordid tears and a sing along. We are losing people here, people are dying. Our response is a cohort of sanctimonious rich bastards talking about their feelings, talking about trying … people are *dying* here. Can we send home the bronze fucking medalists and draft in some goddamn winners please??? How many dead kids is this gonna take?!?

"YOU. You think it's good there's at least someone saying it? Saying what? What are they saying? Universal background checks … ugh, please. Think about it; it's a form of checking and observing, it's not a form of intervention. Gun violence is you saying the room is too hot. Universal background checks is someone handing you a thermometer. I know the NICS was designed by the NRA, but shoring up the system we have won't make a dent on the statistics. Research is telling us this now. That should be getting done any who, not announced on a podium waiting for a round of a-fucking-pplause.

"And assault weapon bans … I mean, this just takes it, this just takes the fucking bait. Does the media report on life? Or does life perform what the media would like? Out of all the lives lost, out of all the gun deaths in a calendar year, why are we chasing a percentage of the problem? Then the one time the Cremodats get a chance to swing at that one, they gut the policy and put it on a timer like they were boiling a fucking egg.

"It's just *bullshit*. It's more empty, more nothing. Declaiming things that make us look good but don't actually help anybody at risk. What kind of sickness is it to *pretend* to care in the face of child mortality? Maybe that's the start, maybe we're too aggrandizing of ourselves. Maybe if we took the collective hit of realizing how little legitimate care there is, that would propel us into action. Compel us into action. People are compelled away from things not towards them. We are far too romantic about us on far too little evidence.

"And it's the pissing screen culture man, it's poisoned everything. Performative this, performative that. People don't have feelings on what matters anymore, they just announce feelings they think they should have in hope of retweets, likes, validation. Everyone wanting to be the next thing and the new thing because everything else is forgotten or thrown away. Make everyone a 'customer' then wonder why the world gets selfish and entitled. Been thirty abortive years of this empty crap. Thirty years of selling ourselves down the river. Thirty years of shrugging at the vulnerable. Thirty years of empty policy by wannabe patron saints. Thirty years of impotence on a matter of life or death."

Kyle had a look on his face that breathed disturbance: cheeks tensed, a wince and gritted teeth. He had long put down his gravity bong. Everything got quieter. It dawned on me how long I had been talking and how much I'd raised my voice. I slowly got up and made my way towards the door. I sheepishly thanked Kyle for offering me his place, but I'd recognized I should be going. Poor Kyle, he seemed a nice guy, he didn't deserve that. I wish I hadn't shouted at him.

19

MAIN STREET IN THE EARLY hours was pleasant enough. I mean my jaw was near jittering off the bottom of my skull but the place looked nice. A "leaf peeper" is what locals may have referred to me as. That being said, glances down side roads even this late at night showed the legendary potholes of VT. A few I looked down; the first one you could have used a fireman's ladder for. The second one looked like Satan's Alcatraz-style get out from hell. The third, non-descript wildlife was attempting to make a home out of. A low, agitated growl shortly countered my curious nosing. I leaped back onto the sidewalk swiftly and for the first time in my life, I found myself grateful I wasn't a car.

Burlington was soft. The bricks beneath your feet. Plenty of warmly-lit and decorated stores with traditional red and white awnings. As the cold hit my cheeks without remorse, my eyes took in Church Street in the early hours without a soul or sound to disturb. Doing a full rotation, I realized there wasn't a building in sight towering over anything. A world that had been constructed for people, not a pouring metropolis convulsing from every angle. The only remotely tall buildings were state or church related, not an ominous corporate brand in sight. An unfriendly tightness hit the back of my throat and I took a seat on one of the several benches. I got all wet around the eyes … the hell did I never move to a place like this and make a damn life for myself?

As my eyes got hot and wet, the air got cold and still, and I began sniffling as snowflakes fell playfully all around me. My field of vision filled with flecks of delicate white as I slowly took in the stores around me. The one behind was a bespoke maple syrup store, the one ahead was a small, box-like craft beer place, and there were at least three retailers of hiking gear. My hands had began to sting with sub-zero settings. I wrapped them up in my jacket and could see my breath punctuating the falling flakes. Vermont was a place to wear several layers and I didn't have 'em.

I had always heard that surviving the cold was a matter of the mind. That if one could regulate their breath and keep the mind away from numbing, stinging extremities, the cold could be ridden. To let one's mind wonder away from a jittering jaw and shuddering of breath and to focus on one thing. One detail, one picture, one scene, one story. It's strange, when you're surrounded by snow all your mind wants to imagine are snowy landscapes. I didn't know much of Vermont. I had only one story about VT, although I was right in the spot where it more or less began.

I heard a story of a guy who made it in Vermont. He was working class, a war baby, a "boomer" dare it be said, raised in Brooklyn no less. He soon found himself a student of Chicago and in the bubbling cauldron of the '60s, a sweet Jewish boy became a civil rights activist. The university desegregated their campus and after several anti-war sit ins, the '70s produced an electoral candidate standing for governorship of a Democratic Socialist party. Yet to leave his thirties, the following decade had our Brooklyn boy become the Mayor of Burlington. He fought off gentrification for a national first in non-profit affordable housing. The decade came to an end, but the man had only begun.

America was building towards the culture wars at the start of the '90s, the boy from Brooklyn had other plans than war. In '91, the House had its first independent representative in 40 years. He voted against the future fall from Glass-Stegall, opposed war in Iraq and the Patriot Act. This guy didn't mind making his colleagues uneasy; Irupblecans, Cremodats, he only lambasted them for sucking up to the rich and wealthy. Being a representative was small fry for this guy, a Senator was in the making.

He is still up there, you know. In 2014, he made the ACA cover community centers out in small towns. He's reforming the Department of Veterans Affairs, so those that come home never walk alone. He stood against the Wall Street bailout and demanded that the Fed be audited so Americans would never face a housing bubble indignity ever again. His time in the Senate was given 100% approval from the NAACP and the NHLA. He's one of the few popular politicians in the country, this guy, I think you can see why. He's now 72, he ain't fresh or new, certainly not a young man, but he does have a plan, one that he's seeing through. Some might say, he ought to be president someday …

I woke to a nudge and a shocking crick in my back. My breath was incredibly tight, like I'd developed asthma during my night bench sleep. When I looked up, there was a lady a lot more wrapped up than I was. She was Black and had gone with the blonde weave from what could be made from the inside of her puffer jacket. Words had left her lips but I didn't hear them in my initial disorientation.

"Excuse me, sir," a concerned voice called. I looked up into full, dark eyes and a worried expression.

"Are you OK?" she said, sounding remarkably genuine. But slept I had, and sitting upright no less. Some of my clothes had a weird morning damp on them, my feet and calves were more frosty.

"You sleep out here, hun?" she asked. My God, I wanted something to take my mind off, I didn't mean to pass out. With an unease I unclenched my hands from underneath my crossed jacket arms. The sight before my eyes was quite hideous. My hands had gone a rude purple and ugly blue overnight.

"Oh sugar, lets get you in," her voice purred in a seemingly more desperate tone. The initial attempt to wiggle my fingers was markedly unsuccessful. All I got was a dull, heavy ache in either wrist. Upon getting to my feet, I was lucky my new-found friend was at hand; I went nearly straight over on my face. My legs were too numbed out for function. I informed the transgender person who was holding me up, that my name was Sam and I asked hers. She said: "Terri." I asked Terri what pronoun she wanted to be referred to with. Terri said: "They." So … they were Terri, and after some awkward hobbling on frozen pavement, we made our way into the Pride Center.

Terri claimed they had come in early that morning as "you never know" who could need help. They said they weren't quite expecting me, however. I informed Terri this was a fair assumption. Unfortunately, understandably, Terri went into some kind of back office after sitting me down with a coffee next to a radiator, and came back with homeless shelter materials. They were a little taken aback by my animated denial of my apparent homelessness. Terri was a warm soul. They sat down in front of me, they tilted their head and tried to re assure me I was not the first taken in from the cold by the Pride Center. Terri had been very kind to me, and I was fearful I'd be taking advantage of their politeness.

Looking around the center, it was a truly lived-in space, decorated wall to wall by its inhabitants. Like a house given the adorning of a family of many years, a home. I glanced around the display boards and posters about; there were schedules and programs in an array of colors. It looked closer to a possessed disco ball than the rainbow analogy applied to this community, but nevertheless, the thought crossed my mind, this place must really come alive when people are about. There were at least 40 acronyms per display board but I got most of them.

"Terri?"

"Um hmm."

"What's … QTPOC?"

"You're lookin' at it. Queer and Trans People of Color. Ta-Da!" Followed by a hearty giggle.

"It's a beautiful spot you've got here."

"Thank you. We get a lot of input from the community. You warming up?"

I was. The coffee wasn't bad at all either. Some vegan-kosher-low fat-halal-organic-dolphin friendly-eco bullshit, but it made for a wonderful cup of joe. Terri eyed me up. Warm eyes, though playful eyes, they were definitely trying to figure me out, but it was with a degree of gentle.

"Sam?"

"Yuh …"

"If you're not homeless, whatcha doin out there?"

A silence arrived that couldn't be penetrated for the next full 15 seconds. My gaze found its way to the floor on a dramatic angle. I had a clear head, but a bit too clear as a single thought could not be found. Furthermore, any impulse to speak was met with a kind of involuntary mute.

"Hell-ooooooo …" Terri prompted me to break from a visible dissociation.

"I came here to see you."

"Me?" Terri's eyes got rather large and the tone was one of concern.

"I mean, a representative of the Pride Center. Not you, personally."

"Well, shoot."

"I work in research and … er … I am looking at gun violence. I couldn't help but notice a recent article—sorry, articles—covering the murder of trans people, and I wanted to speak to the community."

"You not from Burlington, are you?"

"Na."

"Came here for the Pride Center?"

"Well, biggest transgender community in the country, outside of DC."

"I think about that old saying 'if a tree falls in the woods …' you know?"

"Right."

"Sam. I can't even begin to tell you the level of vulnerability," Terri said. I heard their voice wobble, then it was Terri staring at the floor, Terri looking haunted. They soon came back into the room, though, and began with eloquence:

"I could tell you what stands in the way of anyone *seeing* this vulnerability. LLE doesn't keep its records all that great, Federal records have to be voluntarily given. Between these two things alone … we have aftermath and summary, we don't have a finger on the pulse of the amount of harm done here. Law's still a while from having transgender people's backs, only 20 states outline gender and sexual discrimination on their books. So … if the institutions don't have your interests then it's … down to the people.

"See. I said local law enforcement doesn't keep record so great, and that's hugely affected by the people enforcing the law. We see case after case of police misidentifying people with their birth-assigned gender. This is informed by people again. Some people haven't come out to their relatives, people can use the wrong pronouns in the search for a person. The whole crime scene and the process is informed by the choices of people. There is a study saying that since 2013, half of transgender murders have been committed by a close friend or loved one. So, often it's hard to tie up any loose ends as perpetrators against transgender people get to claim 'panic defense' and almost always walk free. It's down to the people."

There was a softness to the mood in the room, it was delicate. They'd outlined a lot of problems, a lot that felt chaotic and dark without easy answers. My masochism invited a peer behind the curtain.

"And the amount of this damage caused by guns? That's the part I look at. That's why I'm here."

"Did you come here for numbers?"

"Ideally, but I'm guessing with what you said, there's no access to anything reliable."

"I can give you figures but there could be more, we can't possibly know."

A brief silence fell between us. Morning was coming up in Burlington, and all the smiles on the walls and the color that filled displays felt cardboard. The whole building had a vulnerability all of a sudden.

"We have our gun violence prevention policy outline if you wanna look at it?" Terri asked. They got up and made their way over to a wall filled with files and started sifting through a binder of materials. I took a sip of the wonder brew Terri had made for me. A sinking feeling arrived in my stomach that wasn't down to the jet fuel I was slugging. My brow furrowed; I got the same agitation I had with Sharon in Mass, a sense of people being targeted and a gaping whole in my idea that—

"Here we are." Terri handed me the proposal. Opening the document was a page-by-page equivalent of smelling salts. Demilitarization of Police. Stand Your Ground. No Fly. Restrictions. My heart hit an uneasy pound. The warmth in my face rose to a heat. It was Boston the sequel. My eyes opened in an unblinking wideness. I must have been red as a traffic light.

"You warming up!" Terri said enthusiastically, oblivious to the internal chaos. I managed an odd agreeing nod that produced an involuntary affirmative groan.

"What do you think?" they implored, warmly invested.

A hole beneath my feet may well have opened as I covered my lost ass in a strange performative baritone.

"I think you've got some strong stuff here." I boomed like an exec injecting HGH into his own ball sack every morning. "I'll be glad to relay this back to the folks at the think tank in DC."

I got up to my feet. An ungodly crack thundered through the room causing Terri to levitate a foot in the air. My back had angled out even further.

"OH SHIT! *ARE YOU OK?*" Terri yelped, clapping a hand over their mouth.

Was I OK? I looked like a snapped fishing rod. My back had completely spasmed out. It came upon me. I had no choice. I'm still a person, you know?

But I had gone far right.

"I'll be fine," a voice croaked out of me, as the very exec from earlier now sounded like they were now two weeks into a rehab stay. Craning over the desk my coffee sat on, I took a last swig. It was a disaster resulting in a coughing fit till my nose ran. Giving Terri a goodbye nod, I waddled out of there like a trashed *Richard III* and popped an OxyContin the moment I hit the street.

20

DAYLIGHT STRUCK ME IN A near vampiric moment. As I swayed my way across the sidewalk, I'm certain I tipped over a stroller and at one point had to be hauled out of the road. Walking with the posture of a velociraptor does change one's relationship with gravity. The first 'Contin didn't do much for me, which was a disturbance I could live without. I popped another one in broad daylight, making a couple sitting outside a café drop their cutlery. Richard III meets Dracula was not particularly fit for public consumption. In a zig-zagging swagger, I meandered towards Perkins Pier with half a mind to throw me the fuck off it.

My kaleidoscopic vertical flail meant I soon found out Perkins Pier is for boats. Despite the deluge of embarrassment flooding through my veins, I didn't genuinely want to attempt water in my given state. Operating heavy machinery was another I could give a miss; however, a seat wasn't a bad option. It wasn't just the broken back and the painkillers, I could feel underneath the blur what had struck me sitting opposite Terri. A dark rumbling well opening at the pit of my stomach, accompanied by a tightness in the chest and a foreboding sense something horrible is on approach. In diagnostic terms, anxiety. In internet terms, FOMO. I swayed on towards the fishing pier; I could make out folks sitting on benches.

The bench was one of those early 20th century styles, curved-off austere steel strips shaped into a rounded inviting seat by the water. It had the misfortune of being graced with my turtle on its shell impersonation. Fumbling through my jacket I found the policy leaflet Terri had handed me. In my blur, I must have grabbed the thing in some weird attempt to cover the panic. I unfolded the scrunched article and unraveled the first page. "Gun violence prevention from a social justice framework." Terri's earlier explanation echoed in my head. "Queer and Transgender Persons of Color." Staring across Champlain half out of breath, I was recuperating what the last few hours had been. Then the article that led me here flooded back, the Black face staring up in the photo. My blind spot with a blackness to it.

The Save Lives, Save Guns approach needed a revision. I was no longer swayed. The sky was clear above me, only light wisps of cloud permeated a gentle blue. I needed to take this to the movement, the PAC. There was a grim sense emanating that taking this to an NAACP representative would be an ugly tipping point. Craning my phone out of my jacket pocket, near death of battery, I phoned Adam.

"Yello."

"Adam, we need to talk."

"My sentiments exactly. *When shall we three meet again? In lightning, thunder or in rain?*" he crooned excitedly.

"Cut that shit. I'm heading to the Southern Poverty Law Center. I'm good for a flight to Alabama from Vermont right?"

"What the fuck are you doing in Vermont?"

"Just answer the question."

"Yeah you can fly down. So meet ya in 'bama?"

"Go for the hotel nearest the airport. Send the word on to Andros. No action is required right now, OK? Don't go ahead with anything; let's meet, let's talk. I'm learning a lot here and—let's get back to the specifics, forget the plugging," I implored, sounding more desperate than I wanted to admit.

"Sure buddy. We're in a good position. I'm not your policy guy though, you know that. I'm looking at numbers and the numbers are looking—"

"Adam. Listen to me. Numbers can wait. I'm gonna stop by you guys before heading to the Center. Let's review where we are at. I haven't seen figures for a little while, we need to get our heads together on this."

"Aye aye, cap'n. Do you need expenses for the flight over?"

"What?"

"For the flight? Do you need your travel covered?"

"Covered? From what? From who?"

"From the PAC."

"Oh Jesus, no. Adam—"

"Alright kid, drop ya text when we get to the hotel. See ya in a few hours!"

"Adam!"

He'd hung up. I was no longer in a position to just be flopping on a bench like a displaced sloth.

The slide of old leather didn't help as the car door held me up in the back of the cab. My face was slushed against the window as Burlington floated by. A phone screen could be my only company at the time. Against better judgement, I checked the Twitter account: 2.3 million followers had been amassed. A huge inhale of breath lolled me sideways against the door. Staggering were the responses. Whatever the hell this thing was, it inspired people to quote back, no matter their take on the issue.

"That's the only thing that matters—saving lives."

"All this feeling and anger and hurt that's come from this … made almost no difference in federal gun control laws. How little do we have to watch the Hill do?"

"If we're serious about gun control, we need to get serious on compromise."

"Another tragedy all too predictable: When will this country choose to protect children instead of guns?"

"The most messed up thing—these school shootings have had virtually no effect on our elected officials."

"My gut feeling—pro-gun or anti-gun, when that gunman was prowling with his rifle, I bet one of those victims wished they had a gun on their person."

"There's a lack of *care* in Congress, that's why we never see any worthwhile response or action."

"There's a sickness in this country if children are the victims of gun violence, but are there even words, when they're also the perpetrators?"

"This is a small state. We have community here, we know one another. Knowing our neighbors is something we take pride. How in God's name has it come to this?"

"This standout issue of importance to millions of Americans—the issue of guns—leaves me dumbfounded when all we hear from people who think they should be president are empty reforms we've been hearing for at least 20 years."

I reached into my coat pocket only to find no more 'Contin. My breath seemed to have been vacuumed out of me and I instantly burst into tears. The cab was approaching Burlington Airport departures. I may have been a wreck and in pain and all that shit, but goddamn it, something had to be done. My thumbs worked the phone screen and I hit another tweet out to the 2.3 million legion:

Bloodshed was once borne by the brave, for the best of reasons.
Now it's only by the basest, for the worst.
#MakeAmericaSafeAgain #SLSG

The cab pulled up. I wrangled out the back wailing like a Harvey Keitel '90s film, and hoped a coffee onslaught and a freshen-up in the gents would make me presentable enough for flying.

21

B EING A WALKING CRANE IN silhouette earned me an extra seat from a stunned looking lady at the ticket desk. My hours in the air were spent in stages of discomfort. The opening 30 minutes were just getting through the ascending rumble of the plane, which didn't do anything for me. Burrowing with luggage, blankets and pillows, I'd constructed a mound on the seat beside to support my lopsided body. I got a couple of whiskeys from the service cart, and when it passed for collecting empties, I managed to sneak a couple of 'em without the hostess seeing. A warm melting sensation slowly began to fill me; how I was sitting didn't matter anymore, and I soon woke up in The Yellowhammer State.

The sun's glow illuminated all below upon stepping out of the airport. As the warmth rained over me, my phone rumbled with Adam's message informing me the hotel address. I hailed a cab and the moment I announced the destination, the driver gave me an odd look. He told me it was but a walk away. Google informed me of the 20-minute stroll, and I soon found myself outside a Holiday Inn in Birmingham. Well, at least I didn't need to be *too* concerned about us overspending any of the PAC money.

Opening the hotel room door, I was nearly knocked on my ass by a roaring white cloud. It dawned on me the cloud didn't end. The cloud was thick, suffocating smog engulfing the entire hotel suite. It had an entire eco system of clouds following it, floating round the room. What kept me in there was the smell, it was tongue pleasingly gorgeous. Suddenly, Andros stepped from the fog, becoming visible only at the last second. I mainly made out his hoodie through a squint and initially thought a Jedi Knight was approaching.

"Hey, thank God you're here, man. Your guy Adam, he's out of control, man. I'm not joking. Everything—"

He exploded into a coughing fit. Andros' long limbs waved clear for some oxygen while he regained his composure. "He takes everything too far. I don't think he respects himself."

It was a fair assessment but I still had one burning question: "What the fuck is going on here?"

"Adam bought shares in a hyper cannabinoid vape start up with the funds from the PAC."

"OH FOR CHRIST SAKE!"

"I know dude, I know. He's got—I don't know what to say ..."

Andros took a long pause with a searching gaze into the smog. He turned to me, face serious and unblinking.

"I think it's best if we just take him out."

"Take him out? You join Mossad since we last met?"

"SAM, HE CANNOT BE HUMAN."

"I can see why you feel that way but he's done a lot for this project. Where is Adam anyway?"

"On the bed, vaping."

"Hey Adam!"

"Leave him! He's asleep, it's like a T-Rex—you don't wake it."

"You said he was vaping."

"Oh yeah, in his sleep. Look for yourself, he got an idea of using the tape."

Delicately, I slowly plodded my way further into the smoke. With no more than three steps, the sight of Andros had vanished and I'm pretty sure I heard an owl hoot. Feeling like I was suffering from a blindfold, I just kept plodding and putting my arms out ahead of me. Creamy pistachio vape filled my lungs as I plodded till I hit something. My hand felt the corner of the bed where a post would be. I shuffled my way round to make out the fountain of vape that was Adam. Looking like a mummified version of himself, once getting close enough, I saw he'd duct taped six vapes in his mouth. He was drenched in sweat, and there was a piece of paper beside his head lying on a pillow alongside a pack of cigars and a lighter. The page torn from a note pad read:

WHEN OUT OF BATTERIES,
REMOVE,
REPLACE WITH CIGARS,
LIGHT

"Andros, you can't take this—"

I screeched loudly. The Jedi Knight bastard had materialized right next to me.

"Andros, don't ever do that again! Look, you can't take this seriously, just—we'll talk to him."

"No man, na, na, na listen. He is too charismatic. Who do you think taped him up so good? I don't even ethically agree with that and I still did it. His charisma is dangerous and seriously misguided. Man, he crowdfunded a $19.4 million real life search for the Holy Grail after a coked-up *Indiana Jones* screening. He's not normal. He's just got an ungodly ability to sell people shit. He's Pandora's box, pal, and I'm all for a cattle prod in the back of the neck. Let's take him out, dump him on a train to Nebraska."

"Jesus Christ, Andros. We are not 'taking people out.' What are you talking about $20 million in crowdfunding?"

"I'm not joking—he set up five laptops and got a giant Google Hangout going and made some kind of deal. I can never understand what he's actually talking about, you?"

"Never. It's just always worked out in my favor."

"So, he's conducting this mass Hangout, starts a bidding war across six bank accounts and around 30 parties. He bids them all adieu then turns to me; he says, 'Right, we're 20 million the richer but on your life, don't ever be seen in Brazil or China.' He then chucks all the laptops out the window, growling, 'The fuckers can never find these' and 'Don't ever get a webcam again.' He starts rabidly vaping, saying shit like, 'Can you cancel ownership of your kids like Netflix? I think they'd be better off without me.' Then … his eyes lit up like a demon and the gab *really* got going. At first I thought I was hearing out a suicide plot, then he sold me into complying with the vapes."

Well, at least that explained the pile of shattered laptops a little way off the hotel entrance. Looking down at the vaping semi-corpse of Adam, I couldn't help but consider, I really didn't know a thing about him. His name was Adam, he had fathered children at some point, he liked raising funds … that was it. My mind had a more pressing immediate matter.

"What about the note?"

"The note?"

"Yeah, the one on the pillow there. The note about the cigars."

"Yeah?"

"Who wrote that?"

"I wrote the note too."

"You wrote the note?"

"Yeah. I wrote it."

"But the note could *only* have been written for me or you."

"I KNOW MAN, I KNOW!"

So, against Andros' advice, we woke Adam. He was not pleased we'd bothered, yet became quite chirpy upon seeing my face. Before this moment, I had no idea, but Adam did in fact have a hairpiece. Sitting up in front of us on the bed, clearing a couple clouds of vape fog, he unscrewed his hairpiece and placed it beside him. Akin to a Darth Vader helmet removal, it was one of the most disgusting-cum-fascinating things I'd ever seen. Adam crawled towards the end of the bed, then out of sight into the fog. Standing there with Andros, it felt ominous till we heard the mini bar door clink and Adam crawled his way back.

"So. Have we got reason to celebrate or have we got reason to celebrate?" he declaimed, while he handed me a mini JD from the fridge.

I declined. "Hey pal, I think we gotta do a little clean up first before we do any celebrating, wouldn't you say?"

"Oh FUCK that! They got cleaners ..." Adam belched indignant.

"I see your logic there pal but um ... they don't expect a debauched vape consulate when they come to change the fucking bedsheets. We gotta think about how we get all this shit out of here without alerting the local authorities."

"Distraction. I say we call in a fake bomb threat on a local kindergarten."

"How do you summon the worst possible options with no encouragement?"

"*We're winning hearts and minds!!*" he roared, to literally no one.

Adam was looking increasingly awake after his whiskey; he said all this staring down at his phone, avidly swiping away. Between the screen's backlight glow and his swiping, Adam increasingly became the clearest picture in the room. He looked up at me.

"Now take a look at this, kid, you won't regret it," he purred, grinning like a movie star.

Handing over the phone, Adam was as clear and as calm as he'd been since we met. This is a person I would never describe as serene but he looked close at the time. He lit up a fat cigar between his teeth at the side of his mouth and said to me: "You're gonna love it."

The first sight was the Instagram account handle 1nOnlyTDHaklin.

"Oh Jesus, Adam, you're obsessed. It's like you've fallen in love with the guy. Not Della Haklin, not again, not again. Do you need to go to Iowa and make it official?" I implored, handing the phone back to him instantly. Yet, Adam's hand pushed back mine.

"I told you," he said firmly, his wide eyes staring up into mine. "You're gonna love this."

A grey circle with an arrow in its center filled the black phone screen. I gave Adam one last glance and pressed play.

Instantly, I was taken away to a tropical island, a beach somewhere. Smooth silky legs floated across the white, sun-scorched sand, in a slow motion run. Smiles and dazzling smooth faces soon accompanied these legs on the screen; they were all models, all terribly good looking people. I'd seen worse sights. A sprawling, gorgeous, sunlit tropical landscape filled the screen from endless angles. Then promises soon followed:

"interactive, transcendental," "state of the art, immersion," "the manifestation of dreams," "defying the limits"

The screen faded into an orange tile with a logo of flames. The flames slowly blended into two letters of white embossed onto the orange tile …

"BA"

I slowly placed the phone back in Adam's hand. He was grinning like a feline on a catnip binge.

"So what is this exactly, Adam? I don't know what I'm looking at here."

"Ah, it's a bunch of kids putting a festival on an island somewhere. The internet's going crazy for it. Some guy I spoke to said they were already 50 million down and about a year out of time but I'm sure it'll work out fine."

"A festival … on an island … then why's 'BA' at the end of that?"

"Great publicity no?" Adam near bellowed at me.

"Well … Doesn't it insinuate 'BA' means people are going to be surrounded by models on a tropical island somewhere?"

"Oh I don't see how anyone could get *that* impression. We gotta build hype for this thing you know."

I was close to incensed. It felt like Adam had a selective learning difficulty that only proved operational when it came to my input.

"You haven't listened to a goddamn word I said on the phone, have you?"

"What do ya mean?"

"Don't plug the thing! That's been my message for like the last month. To like fuckin' both of you!"

"This wasn't us. Can't you see? It's growing, man. We didn't do a thing. It was TDH."

"Oh Christ, TDH now? He's TDH to you now, like you two catch up over brewskis …"

"It's his Insta-plug, the whole thing was his idea, he sent me the link this afternoon."

"Well it's his thing, leave him to it. I'm gathering you guys because we need to get towards the specifics and away from fantasy."

"You sure about that?" Adam crooned with a smile across his face.

I could not believe this guy. I snapped: "OK, what do you know that I don't?"

"Look at the account baby … more than we've managed between us." Presidential Adam was back in town.

Praying and hoping I'd get to the point of the meeting between the three of us, I shuffled into my jacket pocket and checked the Twitter account. Then my blood ran cold.

"What the fuck?"

"Breath-taking right?" Adam cooed like he'd witnessed child birth.

It felt more akin to being punched in the stomach than the witnessing of child birth. The account had definitely reacted to what "TDH" had posted. In less than six hours since my last check, the followers had gone from 3 million to 15 million.

"We need to stop this." My voice cracked with tears in my eyes.

Andros seemed to pick up on my distress. "Is there something you're not telling us? Sam, this is what you wanted."

My face was frozen and not a word could be found in my mind to send to my mouth. Adam swooped in to lift the mood once again.

"We got plenty of money coming in. Like, so much—"

"Adam, are you just limitlessly raising funds? What are we gonna do with all this money?"

"I don't know about any of that. I'm trying to get you rich enough for Congress to listen to ya. Or get ya into a Bilderberg meeting."

"Bilderberg? We're not doing some Bohemian Grove illuminati shit here are we?"

"I dunno, we can burn a hooker in a forest if ya—"

"Just shut up."

My head was pounding and that wasn't entirely down to breathing only cannabinoid vape for the last two hours. I needed to get to the Southern Poverty Law Center headquarters and fast.

22

WITHOUT A TRACE OF IRONY, I found myself on a political journey from a bus in Birmingham, Alabama. However, this soon took a distracted insignificance as I clearly was not well. My mood had gone to shit: a depressive blur with no depth of thought available only punctuated by pangs of horrendous anger. A lady in the seat behind me offered me a cough mint, and I gave her a look that suggested she belonged under the tires. Come 30 minutes into the bus journey, I had a hot glow all over my body and almost permanently perspiring hairline. Alabama passed by in the window to my left, and my reflexive reach for OxyContin gave me the missing piece of the puzzle. I'd gone into withdrawal. Figured I'd sleep it off. That was a nice thought. Reality left me closed eyed writhing against the window silently sobbing.

Like life had turned into a hallucinatory hellhole, I got off the Greyhound opposite the Freedom Rides museum in the Heart of the Dixie. SPLC—or the "poverty palace," as I'd heard it monikered over the years—was only a walk away. My stomach growled and every impulse of my body wanted to ravage through one of the numerous waffle places in my sight line. Therapists call that "eating your feelings." At the time, I coulda had a fucking feast. A tense ball in the stomach reminded me of its presence every step. I needed a coffee but I wasn't tired. I needed food but I wasn't hungry. I needed a blanket but I wasn't cold. I needed a shower but I wasn't dirty. I needed comfort but couldn't be comforted. The scraping at the bottom of my stomach was live, sharp and aching: unbridled bottomless craving.

Despite most of my moment to moment being paranoid prangs of glaring out to the nearest whatever, I could take in some of my surroundings. No doubt, as the sun blazed down illuminating Madison Avenue and all its inhabitants, I was clearly in a state capital. One street sign told me the Supreme Court was a turn away, another that the Department of Labor building was ahead. Seemingly each way I looked were granite archways and fluted columns. A clearing to my right appeared, and there was the capitol building, its visible dome and neoclassical white stone making up the pantheon it was made to represent. Then not far behind, the First White House of the Confederacy. I am glad the Union won; the place looks like a bed and breakfast started up by somebody's grandparents.

Barely a couple of streets away I was approaching the location of the SPLC HQ. The initial sight of the place made me think I'd got it wrong. A towering modern architecture structure with a faux curve for its front, made of dark reflective steel and spotless large windows. Why did the SPLC make everyone imagine a group of driven, sleeve-rolled-up lawyers, chain smoking in a dingy back office early hours in the name of the right thing? This looked corporate enough to be on the stock exchange. Once in eyesight of the front entrance I could see the sign telling me this was the place. I'd contacted someone for a meeting and I was lucky to find a gentleman willing to talk with me over a coffee. Even over the phone his time sounded limited.

Having made my way up the entrance ramp, the stifling air of a surveillance environment descended upon me. The last couple of steps up to the main entrance left me quaking with anxiety and unease. A heaving, muscular tank of a man in a sprayed-on security officer's uniform occupied the landing I was yet to traverse. He may have been only six foot two, but from the bottom of the steps up against my short ass, he could have been about ten foot ten. His head was a near featureless square block on top of a frame bigger than my first apartment. When looking for a face, I only found two dark lines on a blank surface, a short line at bottom for a tiny pout and a slightly longer line above for a frown.

"How can I help you?" *Pixar* incarnate said.

"I have a er … meeting with … Derek Thomas," I croaked in utter short male intimidation.

"A meeting with Mr. Derek Thomas … let me see about that," the horrifying mech-man purred in a Southern drawl. He repeated my request in on the radio, asked for my name and waited till we had it validated. Harlen, as the name badge up in the clouds displayed, stood over me unblinking. Well, unblinking as best I could tell, considering the profound lack of face. We were left standing in relative silence. Had I heard one banjo playing I would have sprinted the fuck out of there.

The crushing tension of standing around with Harlen wasn't good for the soul. Clearly any previous lifetime of social composure was shattered by a lopsided physique and an increasingly sharp painkiller withdrawal. If I wasn't present and feeling like I was soon to be Harlen's appetizer, I was dissociated in imagined arguments with my mom like I was 14 again. It was hardly the best of times, then my mouth ran away again.

"Say, it's one heck of an operation you guys have here with all this security."

Harlen the Mecha Tank took a deep breath in. I was worried there would be no oxygen left for the rest of us.

"Sir, why do people get security at their homes?"

"To protect them."

"Right. So essentially I could be standing in front of any home right now, even your home?"

"I supposed that's true, yeah, indeed."

"Sir, has the KKK ever come to your home and made a half-successful attempt to burn the place down?"

"No."

"That's why I'm standing here in front of all these locked doors and cameras and not in front of your place."

The front doors did open and out stepped a Black guy in a suit jacket and jeans; it was Derek who I'd spoken with on the phone. Harlen's face suddenly developed features metamorphosizing into a cherubim's smile, which nearly gave me a stroke.

"You have a good day now, sir," Harlen wished me in dulcet tones. Derek thanked Harlen, shook my hand, and we took a stroll to a local coffee place he recommended.

Derek was in his thirties and had spent two years working at the SPLC headquarters. He stirred his coffee with a thin strip of plastic from the cashier, and we sat at small table by the window front of the place. He was an Alabaman and had spent years working on the front line of community organizations around the region. His self-introduction was interrupted by his fascination with my bendy-back and general flopping appearance. At one point a single sentence was interrupted by four asks of, "Are you OK?" The situation was not helped by being sodden with sweat. The front of my shirt had visibly darkened. I felt tearful but was holding at least something together.

Derek made himself comfortable, adjusted his square-rimmed glasses and asked in a imploring tone: "How can I help you Sam?"

I was up and it wasn't easy. I told Derek of the PAC; alarm bells were ringing the moment he said he'd caught word of something on Instagram. I said I was there on research. The room got dizzy and my speech vanished from hearing. There was a mumbled blur, and if my mouth was running away again it must have hit the horizon because I didn't hear a damn thing. Returning to the present I was met with Derek heaving with laughter.

His enjoyment of my utter garbage went on for a good 30 seconds. There were two waves. Around the 15-second mark, Derek had taken off his glasses, wiped away tears and clenched his arms round himself to regain composure. He gasped for a bit of breath, took a few deep gulps of water for relief, and let off a couple high-pitched wails. Derek then started laughing again. The whole room thundered with his laughter and he even set off a couple of tables behind us. Yet come around the 30-second mark, his elation died down.

"You came here, to tell me that."

I nodded.

Derek's mood plummeted. Realizing the words that had left my mouth were somehow suggested in anything less than total irony had left him near bewildered. He took a couple of long looks at me before carefully choosing his words.

"This isn't a game that you dip your toes into, give it a try. That place you came to see me at? Most of the staff is white; I'm support staff, I bust my ass in there, go well beyond my job description and I'm support staff. In the walls of the 'poverty palace,' the decision making for the protection of our own isn't dictated by us. We're administrators and support staff … and there's a guy who looks like you in a suit and tie at the top."

He looked me up and down, nearly snorted, then said, "No mention of police or high-risk areas? Not a word on police brutality?"

Derek felt we were done here. He started getting his things together from the table, started putting back on his jacket; he then dismantled my entire visit.

"There is nothing in this to directly benefit persons of color. You're about the 4,000th person to do this. Usually a guy, usually white, usually a spring in his step and heart full of ideals. Comes up, 'I'd like to help. Think I got something of interest.' And y'aint. Never do. Nothing you have stands in the way of a young Black man getting shot, none of it. You, you want to tell people—to turn the gun on themselves?"

He stood up and dusted himself off in a leisurely slow fashion.

"America's beaten ya to it, white boy."

Derek left the building. The waffles I ordered arrived, I managed about two mouthfuls before flopping my way to the bathroom and vomiting violently.

23

I WAS LESS THAN A SHADOW returning to DC. Not wanting to be changed or altered from my course, I went to Birmingham International and bought a ticket out of there before contacting Andros or Adam. Hell, I didn't give a shit for Adam at the time. He was just another rampaging snowball, in a long line of snowballs hurtling down a hill, too far down their descent to be stopped. Slumped in the departures lounge waiting for the gate to open, I was sore all over and had permanently hot teary eyes despite no actual crying. Telling people to shoot themselves was no idea, it never was, and it stood with over 15 million avid-yet-unknowing followers.

My mind set on Andros. He was a guy I'd met in college, one of those people that despite all differences you're only happy they'd come into your life. Andros was pure Cali and a markedly different human to me. Chill, measured, laissez-faire without an ounce of laze. Whenever I was bummed out or broke, or for that matter just resentful or lazy at college, Andros was there. He'd rally me to go get some food and chat the breeze. Or when I'd simply not have a will for study, he'd bargain a few rounds of SEGA out of me and before I knew it we'd be studying any who. He'd never done me wrong, been a solid pal, a good guy—why on earth was he involved in this shit? The one who led me down the path of listening to people not just endlessly plugging them fantasy. I reached for my phone.

The first exchanges between us over text were informative. Andros had bailed on Adam. Adam had left him little choice. The message described Adam having another AC/DC rock out which this time Andros suggested may have been a manic episode. He described Adam standing on the hotel room furniture, drunk as skunk rallying non-existent crowds. Andros decided to bail when Adam revealed he'd be departing via limousine on way to a private jet. When the private jet was revealed not to be Adam's and the proprietor was not revealed either, Andros was heading back to LA. I told him to forget the PAC. I told him it was something I was walking away from.

The messages weren't easy and my texting was accomplished while wiping away my sweat and exhaling away torrents of anxiety. I had genuine gratitude for Andros inspiring the journey I'd taken since meeting him. Doing my best to articulate, I explained as much, yet the bold truth of the matter took all the gravity in the room. I had spoken to America. Even in a demented alternate realm where this Save Lives, Save Guns movement would be possible; it still wouldn't be anywhere near to helping the most vulnerable. Each message felt like a decision, that with each statement I was getting further away. Steadily the texting slowed. Finally, I dropped Adam a message telling him to end the movement and an emptiness filled me.

As I took my seat on the flight, with three attendants asking if I needed any assistance, an all-consuming numb filled the plane cabin. My face squished up against the plane wall and gave me a tiny sliver of the window to look out at the wing. After a few moments, I no longer heard the talking around me. Nature's purest shot of full-strength lithium, dissociation. I'd walked away from the movement. I'd quite clearly lost a job (although a text received from Natalie upon landing would clarify that). I had a vicious withdrawal slithering throughout my being. I had a broken back. I had nothing. As the plane began to make its maneuvers down the runway for takeoff, the resident plane baby screamed to life in an epic crying spree. Within seconds, I was using every muscle in my body to stop myself from joining it.

By the time we landed at Reagan International, my state had visibly worsened. Without willing it at all, sweat-drenched was not enough of a distress signal from my body and rhythmically muttering to myself had developed. The fella sitting in the seat next to mine had spent the flight stoically reading a book, avoiding a moment of attention on me. He was suited, slender. He had an angular face and a short blonde crop of hair. I presumed a model. Could have been a model. Probably just an assistant to somebody in a big building somewhere, knowing modern employment. As the chime of the seatbelt sign went off and a cacophony of metallic clinks rattled through the cabin, my travel companion jumped to his feet and collected his luggage from the overhead. The Redford-alike took me in and in a near silver-screen delivery inquired: "How do I always end up next to the lunatics?"

I had no response and he had no will to sit back down. The clearing of the plane was a welcome moment for both of us.

Whereas the world I'd spent the last weeks and months in was full of vibrant color and the urgency of soul, the return to DC was a punishing, stale monochrome, a world in rote. What filled my eyes was the unwanted impersonal of modern living. Avoid eye contact, headphones in, get to where you've got to be, with all in the way as some irritating obstacle. Airports are unreal showcases of industrial metal and glass and uninterested people. The Uber ride back to my place was slightly illuminated by a driver on a crusade to get a good tip out of me. Damn, I've had some chats in my time, but the pinball pace at which this gentleman careened between subjects was spellbinding.

First it was social conditions of the underclass, then a small detour through theology, a bit of the great Mahatma Gandhi's greatest learnings, who's "tanking" this year, why streaming is ruining movies, only to reach the finish line of the Maryland rent being a sick joke for corrupt landlords. Don't worry, Bob, you've got your tip, I just wish I didn't get a nosebleed-inducing headache in the process.

He wasn't a bad sport. I didn't have the heart or energy to tell him of his exhaustive customer service. I wheezed that the nosebleed was a part of the condition I coined "my back troubles." He dropped me off outside my place and offered to help me. Holding my nose with my head tilted back, I declined and waddled towards my door in a sort of limbo dance kind of movement.

I crashed onto my nest of a bed, unaware of the time or month, let alone the day, and closed my lids to an almighty stinging. Clawing every available cover and rug, I curled up in a crooked ball. Sweating some more, shaking some more, I heavily breathed myself unconscious. The last memory I have of that awful spell was crawling my weak arm out to the bedside table. With drool dripping out the side of my splayed mouth on the pillow, I prodded with shaking fingers and I turned off my phone.

Tech breaks are all-inclusive in DIY rehab.

A dread hit my chest as I laid out flat on the bed. Dear God, I'd been going round the country telling people to shoot themselves as a way forward. My jaw hung like an idiot as I glazed over looking up at the ceiling till it got darker and darker. Then I slept.

24

A BRIEF MEMORY OF WAKING STAYS with me. The turning point for myself. The expelling of demons, an exorcism of the soul. It was a strange quantum that I didn't foresee. Yet this was the turning of a page, a beginning of an end. Without this, I would not have been able to get down all that happened across this wild time.

A limbo within a limbo, unaware of time and barely conscious of place, I found myself staring at the ceiling in my apartment. My entire chest cavity pounded me into the mattress. I was unable to move my body. My eyes would barely open and, when they did, they were wet with tears. Trying to breathe through my nose was a nightmare, it was running only between bursting into sniffles. As I dragged my body up to a half sit, I knew something was wrong, it was my insides hurting and not my back. I got to my feet, feeling riddled with compulsion, quaking on the spot with the will to do something. I gazed round my apartment and felt directionless yet possessed. I'd heard this could happen. I had heard in Swahili it was known as "Mzungu Mavi"… the white guilt had arrived.

Wailing my way around my apartment like a toddler was the start to my day. It was "full man crying" to be accurate: a cascade of snot and incomprehensible high pitched noises as I threw myself against the walls flapping like an idiot. For every frame knocked off the wall, another was put up at breakneck speed. My graduation photo was replaced with a 10×8 of Lou Gossett Sr. The nice pastel flower vase replaced with C.C.H. Pounder. A photo of a campaign I was a part of a decade ago replaced by Pam Grier. The snap I took off the top of the Seattle Space Needle replaced with the late, great Robert DoQui Sr.

After getting through three deluxe-size boxes of tissues and mopping the half-foot of mucus off my floor, I took in my library. I recoiled in horror upon observing that 95% of my books and DVDs were whiter than Maine. My arms swung wantonly clearing the books and DVDs from my shelves. I had put them all in a trash bag and only a black one would do. Despite emotional exhaustion I sailed across the room and flopped on my couch. With urgency that broke half the buttons on my TV remote, I queued up a John Singleton marathon that took me through to the night. Come around midnight, covered in popcorn and flip pads for taking notes, I put on the inauguration of the 44th President of the United States, on loop, for 40 hours. That meant two entire viewings.

For the first time in an age, I had a dream of such vividness I could cognitively remember it. It was one of those disturbing ones that feel hyper real because you dream that you're in your bed woken from a slumber. My eyes opened upon a sense my bedroom door stood ajar, the light from my hallway spilling into the room. I could not remember leaving the hallway light on, and a tremor of panic seeped through me. I began to hear sounds. The gentle pattering of steps came from beyond the door in the hallway. My throat swallowed hard as the door began to slide open at the pace of a snail. This was worse than every horror film I'd spent a lifetime avoiding.

Splayed across the nest like a drunk alopecia sloth, my heart hammered my ribcage in a harrowing powerlessness. The door was fully opened. A short hooded figure, light flowing from behind it, made up a silhouette in the doorway. It was impossible to make out the figure's face. My voice quaking, I said: "Hello." The room responded in thick silence; the figure didn't move, didn't make a sound, and neither could I. The figure started moving towards my bed. A slow calm glided towards me, I began rummaging back whimpering in whimper-dom.

When I saw fingers wrapped over the corner of the bed stand, I clenched my hands into the duvet and shut my eyes tight. My breathing heaved as I heard the figure climbing onto the bed. My hairline dampened as the figure only continued to climb toward me.

My entire skull riddled with tension as I felt the small figure's hands use my legs as terrain. Silence. The pawing plod of this travel on top of me continued till I felt pressure from the knees and then only two points of pressure were on my stomach. Petrified, I slowly opened one eye and the small figure stood over me. Closer, in the darkness, I saw his jacket was puffy, insulated for colder conditions. In pure terror, I peered up from his puffer jacket to inside the fluffy rimmed hood. He had a wispy moustache, then his mouth opened: *"Everyone forgets the Eskimos, you racist bastards!"*

I jolted awake. Sodden with sweat, only the looping of Motown YouTube playlists could regulate my anxiety.

This too came to pass. It must have been around a week or so in, and some Amazon Prime ventures had proven disastrous. The basketball purchase only led to pissed-off neighbors in the apartment below. Attempting to get oneself "moves" for the dancefloor is a pretty arduous matter as a new-found hunchback on a permanent comedown. To add to this, I was dealing with the condition known as "Caucasian." The few times I stacked it following a YouTube video led to the neighbors below thinking I'd got the basketball back out. They threatened to call the police. Then after enough ludicrously grateful handovers with the Chinese delivery driver and realizing I'd very likely survive a police visit, the whiteness monster had swallowed me whole. I was psychologically cemented as a profiteer of the bastards of history: the flail defeated.

Depressive, permanently clammy with perspiration and reeling from the claws of withdrawal and craving, a lot of daytime television was watched. It soon wore thin, however, as it was a reminder of the very madness that led me to starting the bullshit I had. On a particularly duvet and couch based day with incessant rain outside, I sent an email to Magda. It was pathetically whimpering but very befitting of me at the time. To my surprise she got back within the hour. Her response was clear: go away somewhere and be sure to do your exercises every day. She was unaware I was exhausted from a non-stop travel schedule and my back was worse; I hadn't done any exercises at all, just been poppin' Contin.

In a concerted effort to escape an impending crying spell, I hauled myself free from the duvet and off the couch. Reading the email, she'd outlined the exercises, and for the first time in a good while I moved my body appropriately. Within ten minutes, I started feeling brighter than I'd done in months of OxyContin. Life was still a grey, joyless, oversensitive shit, but all of a sudden I'd found my anchor, yoga. My stiffened, pained body was all I had to work with and it became all I did. As the following days turned to weeks, my 10 minutes turned to 15 to 30. I began moving freer and in much less discomfort. That being said, there was a degree of physical pain I was consigned to, and I wouldn't describe my movement as swift. My posture was significantly ... "hunched," putting it mildly. After losing so much mobility from my back troubles, how I looked became the least of my concerns. Eventually, my mind began to clear and I legitimately found myself weighing up Magda's idea of getting away. Not political this time, but for the soul. To clear out my mind and work out what had to be done.

To think, this entire gaping mess could have been avoided had I just *listened to a woman*.

25

I FOUND MYSELF IN SD, BUT no blackouts or delirium this time. Choosing South Dakota as the much needed getaway was one of the best decisions I had made in some time. Its expanse and sprawling nature had left me inspired. I was finally driving my ass around, no more Mr. Important with the tragi-comedy Uber bill. Sure, the rental was way past near death but it filled up with gasoline, connected to local radio and got me where I needed to go. The journey was more like a freewheeling tour to wherever my eye took me without the pressure of a destination or goal. I was a lucky boy.

My days were mainly spent exploring with an ease and excitement. Direction no longer mattered; I was the sponge taking it in from Pierre (that's pronounced "Peer" for those of you not in the know …) to the Ordway Prairie with its pops of yellow and purple florae and roaming Bison, to the rolling green hills of the Wind Cave National Park. There was a sense of being held in Dakota, the first few days going into a couple of weeks; my ignorance of my surroundings was the perfect foil to my lack of direction.

Every day I would be given long, relaxing drives across infinite horizon: green or yellow, rich, deep grasslands and prairies cut in half with a searing blue sky decorated in wisps of white cloud. No screens, no phones, no echo chambers, talking heads, internet bullshit. Only myself, the nature around me and a pad and pen to write down all that had happened over the weeks and months preceding. The fresh air and walks did their job; I don't know if I can say I was better but I was … clearer. I didn't touch a drop of anything; I drank water till every piss was like a firehose come to life. Anytime the back creaked, I stretched, breathed, meditated and when that didn't work, rested. The "nap" became my talent. My back finally had someone doing more than throwing pills at it, it had someone listening to it.

My main mini-residency for a spell was a cabin over in Mobridge by the Missouri River. I managed to wrangle me one off local ad hunting for a couple of weeks. The cabin was a project, largely abandoned; upkeep had not been done, and it needed hours of work to get it into a livable condition. There was something freeing in only having a sink and linoleum flooring as connection to civilized living. The cabin can't have been much more than a 12 by 16 thing, nearly all wood. A couple of small side bedrooms off an open plan, front room couch and kitchen table arrangement. It even had a (don't ask me how) compost-fueled out-house round the back. Over in Norway these cabins are called *hytta*; found on mountains and by watersides, they are an important staple of good living. Simple, barely touched and uncannily cozy; it felt at the edge of the world, and it was mine, all mine.

The cascade of the river's stream made the perfect place to set off from and the most inviting place to return to. Come an evening, I would bring back steaks to barbeque having spent a day traveling on beef jerky, nuts, bananas, and gallons of water. As the orange hue of evening lined the horizon, I'd be flipping the meat on the grill, before skimming stones across the river, trying to perfect my technique. Those evenings never even felt lonely; BBQ and skimming stones became ritual. I was someone dealing with the inner drag of withdrawal and craving; this could cut through all the nature on any given day, but the evenings were untouched … the evenings were my sanctuary. Not having a phone was anxious for all of five days but after … it was near bliss.

My days started with hot coffee and careful routine stretching on the riverbed of the Missouri. There were no curtains to the cabin, daylight was my morning call and that was alright. Once I felt less stiff and woken enough, I'd deck out the hub with pillows to support my back and set out in the rental. I could see from my journeying that East had most of the population and the harvest and I was after more remote spots. Made my way over to Keystone, a tourism town, mainly in search of Mt. Rushmore. Don't get me wrong, it's an awesome thing to see in person, but doesn't Washington look like he's trying to avoid the other three? Like he's been caught at a party standing next to three assholes he doesn't think all that much of. I liked it up there but *the wind*. Shoved my face half way up my skull every time. As if God had sneezed any time a breeze arrived.

I did stumble across a slice of all-America cruising around. South Dakota hosts the biggest motorcycle rally in the world, it turns out. I was unaware of this till one journey had me face a never-ending motorcade of Harleys growling their way through SD. It was an awesome sight; they kept coming, bike after bike, biker after biker. The deafening noise of these big road hogs in unison was breathtaking. I took a spectator's spot at a gas station a little while out; the big burly bikers looked closer to ants from the distance but the engine revs were still only feet away. I remember a glancing thought crossing my mind at the time. Taking in the scale and the unison of this relatively small niche in front of me, maybe I should have been listening to America, not only plugging it shit.

My favorite trip during this period was to Deadwood. Being a diehard fan of the show … *I fuckin' went 'cus I'm a fuckin' fan, alright?* Making my way along the parade of traditional awnings, peeking roofs and sighting the finishes of the tallest points was a bit of a rush. The place felt recoated, re-skinned even, yet still magically kept. I got a real kick out of what was essentially one of the coolest, quirkiest small towns in America. Though I'm sure there was a degree of projection, the place had an aura and atmosphere. Wild Bill Hickok, Calamity Jane and Wyatt Earp once roamed here. At a time when larger than life figures walked the earth, they walked right here.

After some time in SD and spending plenty of quiet time in the cabin, I'd collated a fair amount of what you're reading now. As days went into weeks, my mind was soon occupied with what I'd do when I finally turned my phone back on. Or if I even should turn my phone back on. I was lucky enough life pulled me a weekend spot at a local gas station. It paid peanuts relatively, but it gave me a little dose of structure and routine. Weekend work and log cabin life had formed a new chapter for me. Mobridge and its surroundings brought me a fresh start I didn't foresee and I was reaping the benefits.

I do not want this to gloss over the grim experience called recovery. That has been going on long after the tale you are reading. The preceding does gloss over a fair proportion of miserable crap. Good or bad mood, I'd find myself teary an awful lot of the time, on a weird low level, where there was just a minor lump in my throat that didn't really budge. There was an underlying sense something bad was around the corner most days come around 3. I would dissociate with such automata that strangers would ask if I was still there—like on end of the phone—and I was right in front of them. Yeah, some days my mood would be so foul and aggrieved, I'd drive back to the cabin, having not reached anywhere, only to pass out on the couch, already exhausted. Bludgeoned by the demons of addiction, yet still sober, a score draw: I can't have it your way and you can't have it mine.

Sitting by the cabin under clear night skies brought the PAC back to me. I'd put the radio on low level inside the cabin and stargazed outside to the ambience of the water's flow. Heaviness arrived whenever the PAC and the movement entered my mind. I'd been shown enough to know that this was no longer just about my input. The social media hits and Adam and his goddamn Della Haklin fetish meant people must have been talking. I knew it had to end and I was glad I had taken the steps to tell people that. My trip around America had taught me that saving lives and saving guns in one fell swoop didn't look possible. That at very least there were so many more factors and realities this political charge of mine had not considered. My solution was moot, but a big problem remained. As I took in the stars above me, still quite unsure what to do; I was out, yet there was unfinished business.

26

I N A BID TO DISTRACT myself from the weight of a looming responsibility, the days were spent looking for ways to engage in
the state. Kind of like my once data job in DC, I was looking to
do good and make some little difference in the right way. Weekends
at the gas station making my face an increasingly familiar one led to
locals giving me insight into whereabouts of the state's happenings.
Tip-offs led me West; the more I found myself West, the more I
was exposed to the gravity of the reservations. While the Native
American population lives off tribal land in overwhelming majority,
I was at the home of arguably the two most famous. Day to day my
exploration and locale were slowly creeping towards Pine Ridge.

I had only a little insight when gravitating towards the reservation. I knew that the Native Americans living on reservations
had been neglected by the powers that be for some time. They were
economically disempowered, had high unemployment rates and
despite reservation bans had found the grip of alcoholism hem-
orrhaging communities for decades. In the 1970s, the aboriginal
people of this land found themselves with the highest murder rate
in the country. Furthermore, over time and administrations many
communities had had their land seized, often in the name of defense spending (oh the irony …), only for it to be returned when
the damage had long been felt. There were no grand aspirations for
going to the reservation, but I wanted to be a spare set of hands,
useful. Not just looking around with a voyeur's eyes and not a single

idea in my brain. My late afternoons became filled with correspondence with Native American Aid.

Emails and a couple of telephone interviews led me to shadowing an outreach worker. Her name was Andi; she had been doing outreach at NAA for eight years, having been a regular social worker off tribal land in her previous work. Andi was warm but serious, folksy to an expert degree, someone who could get to the point without the slightest sense of angst. Most of my time with Andi was spent sitting in her van making our way round the reservation, talking all things native. Andi was proud Lakota and told me she'd been waiting many years to have the financial security to work solely for the betterment of her people. Making our way round the reservation, we'd predominantly be talking to locals and occasionally dropping into homes with food support for elderly residents. It was a sight to behold how everyone we met knew Andi and was able to talk in shorthand and openly. Andi's good grace was enough to have me privy to such exchanges; if you were with Andi, you were alright.

Many of the days spent working our way round the reservation usually included a midday pit stop for lunch. My schedule was three days a week, and on those days I only have good memories of being seated at the roadside or in some diner shooting the breeze with Andi. Usually for money's sake we sat with homemade sandwiches; after a while, Andi started bringing two of her own, one for her and one for me. Despite most of my DC living being fueled on homemade sandwiches, Andi's were another caliber. I suspect an observant eye on my dismal efforts had inspired her lunchtime generosity. Andi was a savant of Native American knowledge, particularly about the Rez. Her pride and knowledge in the standing of Native women was remarkable. Around 70% of the reservation's college graduates were women, the same for reservation employment. Andi told me that schools couldn't run without women: nine out of 10 school jobs were held by women. Andi was proud and she had a lot to take pride in.

Those lunches in Andi's van were practically mini-lectures, like the handful of good and inspiring ones you can still vaguely recall from college. Andi was eager to coach me on the importance of building relations and rapport with the locals, with reservation unemployment being around 80%, "people need people," she'd say. Over a mortadella masterpiece, Andi revealed progressive thinking, yet it was all rooted in the traditions of her people. Same-sex attraction and non-binary identification are considered sources of unique perspective and insight, celebrated in Native tradition. The philosophy Andi had was one of unrelenting positivity, not to stare at the bad but to look to what could be done now to mitigate the harm. Andi celebrated like a sports fan when telling me of the $6.5 million nursing home in construction in Whiteclay. The insufficient health care for the reservation and some of the shortest life expectancies in the West had convinced Andi to do work on the ground every day. "If lives of people on the reservations could be made better today in any way, it should happen," her commanding tone would inform me.

She was like a *Rocky* montage personified; where was Andi when I was stuck in a basement in DC ...?

The tired car seats of Andi's van grew to be a familiar comfort. The locals soon knew me as "The Lieutenant" or "LT," a warm rib of my right-hand man/underling status to Andi. I had the good fortune of locals beginning to talk to me as well as Andi. I never found any self-pity off any party dealing with the downside of advantage. They were all open to opportunity, though it was described as a "dried well" by many. Interestingly, the elderly citizens were often talking of the youth with concern; the high suicide rate and the burgeoning gang culture only formed over the last few years. Andi spoke of how inevitably young people go off the reservation looking for employment. Some end up in the hands of those who take advantage of the disadvantaged. It was rare to encounter citizens without alcohol; Andi believed alcoholism had affected the majority of the reservation's families. Sometimes getting back to a quiet spot for lunch in the van was like coming up for air.

As my education and understanding of the reservation and its needs increased, Andi began turning the spotlight on me. How my story had led me to Pine Ridge. There was a plume of unease and embarrassment bringing my truth to Andi. I felt antithetical to Andi and the work she brought to the table. The more I explained, the more I felt antithetical to Native American identity in total— guns, money, drugs, insomnia. Yet, being the warm, mature human she was, Andi only listened with genuine garnered interest, and I felt I had someone to talk to. Avoiding the specifics was carte blanche for me at this point. The movement was started on a demented idea from an unwell person, that was clear as day to me. My problem lay in making sure the thing was put to rest. Making sure no damage was done and bringing those involved to reality that the movement was empty, there was nothing there, nothing to do what it said it could: false promises. My wording to Andi was that I'd let people down working for a PAC, that I'd made mistakes that needed rectifying, not just for my sake but for the cause of gun violence prevention it- self. Thus followed one of the few purely comedic exchanges I shared with Andi. She told me in response to my gripe,

"A man admits his scars."

"I didn't know that was a Native American saying."

"It isn't. I heard it on Oprah."

My haven and rebirth in South Dakota would only last for so long. I think it was a Tuesday and I was driving over from Mobridge to the reservation to meet up with Andi. The car radio soon in- formed me that another national media covered mass shooting had occurred. Around 25 people were dead and double that injured. Once I'd heard the first full report, I turned off that radio and sat in silence. I could feel my mood had been thrown somewhere I didn't want it to be. By the time I got to Andi and we were making our rounds on Pine Ridge, it was clear to anyone near that I was borderline dissociated. I do hold genuine regret over this. On a day I went out to be of service to others I was an empty shell. To the point where the locals could see and were even able to comment, it was that blatant. Andi tried picking me up at one point, or at least giving me a kick in the ass.

"Hey! What's the matter with you? Do you need to go home?"

I declined and told Andi I'd talk to her at lunch. For the next couple of hours of the morning I managed to bring myself to engage with people. Thought it can't have been my most endearing of community support performances; I'd lost my smile and found an engraved frown.

Come lunchtime, I was a balloon that burst. I let Andi know it was the shooting that had got to me. I say "let her know," but it was more like a pissed-off '80s wrestler cutting a promo. Voice raised, thigh thumping, finger extended to point at my invisible foe, I was close to a ranting lunatic. Once I'd expended enough energy to want to breathe again, Andi was shrewd enough to compliment me on my "passion." I could feel a despair crawling over me. It was grim, and I expect a bitterness from my failed venture did not help,

"Let's face it, this country is a plutocracy. It's not that the Black kids getting shot day in day out don't matter, it's not that the white kids getting shot up in schools don't matter. It's that none of it matters till the kids of the important stand to face these vulnerabilities—then we'd fucking see something. If it were the children of the wealthy and powerful in the line of fire, this place would have been made safe years ago. Then, magically, the NRA doesn't matter, the lobbyists don't matter, the money doesn't matter, the gun owners don't matter, the Constitution doesn't matter. An incident with a gun would be a tragedy, not a familiarity. A shock, not the eternal return of the same … and these are the stakes. It's such a horrendous situation, the only supposition left makes me sound like a bloodthirsty, murderous lunatic, and I don't want a *single person shot*. Yet, you're left with the question, if the gated communities cannot be breached and gated communities are there to be reached, then what's gonna change about this place? What's in changing it for those who are safe? That's the dog whistle message to this country; it's violent enough to swallow you whole, but get to the gated communities and that's someone else's problem."

"You speak with a bitter heart. That is in you, not in America."

Andi took a beat. She then took a few more; we would have sat in silence if not for her sandwich. Andi sat chewing her sandwich looking out of her window to the side, before coming back to me: "I can't tell you what to do. Sam, I'm not even sure what it is you want exactly. You talk about this, like, like it is a war. You talk about it like you are going into battle. That's not how I do my work here. That's not how I see it. That's not how I serve my people and the land. I don't think this work is about removing obstacles or shackles or facing opposition; we're trying to be who we are, who we always were, who we were always meant to be."

Andi encouraged me to take my mind away through the work. Just focus on who was in front of me. She told me the answers I was wanting would make their way to me. In what was a distracted and sore day, I got through the rest of the outreach and made my way back to the cabin in the evening. Feeling only slightly less distracted and none the less heavy. The sizzling of steaks did not accompany the evening. I was without appetite and made do with chewing on beef jerky for sustenance. Sat at the river's bank skimming stones, and as the minutes turned to hours I lost the impetus to keep throwing stones out there. It was close to midnight with the moon's glow turning the water into something mystical as the day went over in my head.

A silence arrived. Not a thought struck my mind for a good minute, then what Andi told me finally landed. My god, that's it! I'm American, goddamn it. If there's wrong going down, I don't sit there and let somebody else pick up the load: I'm there. My god, that's why I started this damned thing, people are suffering and I'll be fucked if I'm gonna settle for witness. Like Andi is Lakota: a warrior, a child of the earth, a tribe member, a giver of life. I am American: an idealist, a protagonist, an optimist, a revisionist. Gun violence needs no more suffering to its legacy. Maybe starting something for the right reasons meant I could end it for the right reasons. Life called my number; I was up.

My hand was shaking as, for the first time in a long time, I picked up and turned on my phone.

27

ESPITE WEEKS UPON WEEKS OF progress, my epiphany provided an unwanted rebirth: insomnia. Having turned on
the phone, I'd chucked it on the nearby couch and paced
throughout the cabin. Once the phone was booted up and all the
intelligence agencies in the world knew where it was, a cacophony
began. In what must have been close to a flat 10-minute stretch,
the phone bleated and bleated with message notifications. Text followed email followed missed call followed app notification. About
three minutes into message-mania, I half resigned that the phone
might never properly work again and that I wouldn't be sleeping.
So I made me a coffee.

I'd taken a note pad with me that I'd used since the very start
of the idea back in the shoebox. It was a warn-out A5 thing with
an elastic bind, looked journalistic. Though insomniac once again,
it was an intriguing prospect looking through this document. Or
so I thought. The further back I went reading through this pad,
the more chaotic it got. Well, chaotic is one word. A handful of
Polaroid photos slipped out of the pad. It was of various hotel room
walls with damn near sermons scrawled in stark red lipstick all the
way across them. They were all clearly my handwriting, but I had
no memory of this. I felt numb reading them. The collection of
Polaroids, all of blood red sermons contended:

"*This is child murder and bad begets bad. More kids in schools greeted with metal detectors. More kids on corners hearing gunshots a block away. More kids thinking, 'when's my time?' More kids knowing signature gunfire better than the voices in their neighborhoods. More empty chairs missing SATs. More psyches dented. More youth disbanded. More shitty adults for tomorrow. More peoples and neighborhoods isolated and estranged. More people dragged into the way of the gun* **then believing** *the way of the gun. More gun cancer. More mad doctor garbage. More pro-cancer cancer patients . . .*"

"*Let's add cancer to rid ourselves of cancer cus hey, its only child murder. Let's add it to the fucking house fire. Let's throw a pale of spilled crude oil on it in our cannibalistic gnawing appetite for waste. Let's add it to the bill. Let's throw it on the tab. Let's not spare an expense. Let's add it to the bill that will never be paid—America. More of the same. More of the never change. More slogans and podiums. More pissed off public. More unanswered questions. More posturing. More conflict. More confusion. More freedom. More self-worship. More consumer trends. More convenience over reality. More choosing dollar signs over* **the light in a child's eyes** *. . .*"

"*Sanitized eyes. When the news shows 6 hours of missiles flying and dropping bombs but not one dead body. When we show how violence goes down but never why. When we have worthy victims feverishly covered and unworthy victims never to be shown. When we scream at the world to correct their atrocities but don't have the heart to take on our own. When there's lives being lost and nobody does anything. When America becomes a tanking reality tv pilot drowning the world in its static. More NOTHING. How much more is more nothing? Void, vacant, chasm. Darkness lined with empty bullet shells.*"

I put down the A5 pad like it was the tome from *The Evil Dead*. It was hard to reconcile the jarring rage surging across most pages of this "note pad" with where I found myself at the time. Yet, this was the first time I'd been given a reflection of me in the months previous. A gargling fear started to rumble through me. It was clear as day I'd been unwell. At the time of putting this all together, I was not on the planet. Where the hell had my head been, and what the hell was wrong with me? What mad psycho goes around promoting the idea people should shoot themselves … *AS A SOLUTION!?!?!*

The 10 minutes of downloading the messages was up, and I had taken a few slugs of coffee. The phone had stopped vibrating its way around the couch, and I was good to interact with it. I didn't have time to read every last email and message as it was approaching the 800 mark. The phone itself tipped me off about how long it had been turned off for. I had to enter the time and date settings for it upon reboot. My first call was to drop a text to Adam, who'd left the most messages, telling him to call me. Initial glances through the missed messages were informative. The good news was I was back in the game and knew I had to be informing everyone about what had gone wrong with the PAC, about how it started from the right place but its final product was dangerous, loose and base. How if people wanted to see gun violence changed for the better, following #BA and the Save Lives, Save Guns PAC was not the way. The bad news was, despite making it abundantly clear to Adam the thing needed to be retired and shut down, this had not happened.

Speaking of the Devil, the phone began vibrating in my hand, a call alert came on the screen: the man himself, Adam.

"WHERE THE FUCK HAVE YOU BEEN?"

"You know … some people say 'Hello.'"

"Seriously, I've got a missing persons profile on you in 10 different states!"

"I told you I'd be away for a while. I told you to stop the PAC. How's that going?" I asked, knowing full well I was about to hear something I wouldn't like.

"Look kid, you were looking pretty fried. Time off, sure. As for stopping the PAC, we were in growth; I couldn't stop it *then*. You oughta come see where we are now; we're on a whole other plane to when you left."

The only redeeming feature of this grim exchange was it outlining my plan. I was sure I'd be rolling back into town to put a nail in a coffin. I needed to explain to people why it had to be stopped. Now it was much more urgent; the damned PAC hadn't been stopped and that couldn't wait a single moment. Adam was no longer someone to leave in charge of the task. It was up to me; I had to play it smart.

"All right, get me back in the game then, send me where you wanna send me."

"So … you're on board?"

"Tell me where I gotta go, Adam."

"Right!" Adam said, bursting into life. "There's an OGP governor who's been asking to meet you for weeks now. Can you get your ass to Kentucky?"

"I'm following orders, Boss."

"That's the spirit, kid. Drop me a message when you arrive and let me know how it all goes. I'll send you the address now, OK?"

"Sounds good."

"OH, this is GREAT! The old team back, our MVP back on the roster! The founding father himself! You won't be disappointed. I promise."

The call ended and the task in front of me was daunting. My mind was attached to the uncomfortable detail I was being sent to see an Irupblecan governor. Yet there was a determination I hadn't had in forever; my drive felt pure, not tinged with anxiety. This thing was ending today, and it was up to me. I was clear. Better than I'd felt in an age. I had a purpose, not a delusion. I was my very own avenging angel ready to tear down my empire of dirt. I got the rare opportunity to put my own Frankenstein monster out of business. I made a call to Andi to let her know I had to get back to the gun violence work, and I promised returning to SD was all I wanted, and I meant it. Then once I'd basin washed and changed, I got into my rental and headed for Sioux Falls Airport.

The flight east would be just under four hours. Enough time to get enough done, check the messages, take a nap, rehearse in my head what needed to be said and how it should be said. Probably even enough time to lie down where possible on the plane and keep my back stretched. It was early hours, the airport wasn't in its full rhythm of human traffic. I had a little while before the gate opened. I'd brought the A5 rage diary/evidence file for something to write down thoughts on. After spending a fair chunk of time ambling in between stretching my back, a non-ideal mix of curiosity and boredom bought further reading of it. A little ditty that took up a few pages:

> *Reduce discourse to 280 characters*
> *So a 16-year-old gets 100 million followers*
> *So 1 sports team outspends 52 countries*
> *on defense …*
> *So 1 athlete's valued at 220 million*
> *The cost of raising 870 lives till the age of grown*
> *21.*
>
> *Speculation, consolidation, Inflation, stagnation*
> *Subsidize, minimize, Acquisition, recession*
> *Rally slowing, downturn growing,*
> *reform, merger, free markets, enterprise*
> *But not for everyday*
> *gals and guys.*
> *Sub-prime, blue chip, Gold standard, pump-n-dump*
> *Stock sale, junk bond*
> *Managing, executive, Assistant, vice, chief operating–*
> *Adjective …*
>
> *Spreadsheets, stats, charts, graphs, presentations,*
> *Jpeg, img, pixels, doodles, animations.*
> **A world replacing words with numbers**
> **Plays monopoly money with meaning.**

So buy to get by, to sell, to grow,
Worker bee,
incarnate anxiety.
Desperate drone/whore,
Always want more
And it's never enough.
Want, want, want,
From a sweat shop safety net,
Then your needs, needs, needs,
Are never truly met.

More things, more stuff.
Bright, shiny, plastic,
Flashing, flickering, never-thing …
So sell,
Sell your life, Sell your image
Sell your sex, Sell your past
Sell off your dreams
In patents and IPs,
to consume like a vacuum.

More tweets, likes, comments, trending, hashtags, viral, following—
For the great data kidnap
For boardroom welfare,
For tech savvy, slick suited, wise guys.
Do not subscribe
Do not submit… This form
("Your feedback" isn't needed,
Their "appreciation" is full of shit.)
-USER ERROR-
Welcome to the "No World Order" …
I don't want your time. I don't want your money. I don't want
your opinion, favor, approval or vote.
I want your soul.
Because the suffering are our own,

And in a world of permanent distraction,
The lights are on and no one's home.

I know, I started this book talking about a "breakdown," but this A5 pad's contents were breakdown in bloom. Having got to the end of another regrettable reading session, I was practically heaving with unease. Sitting in departures I followed breathing relaxation techniques I'd mastered in SD. Only focusing on the inhale through the nose and exhaling out the mouth. With a busy mind like mine, sometimes you can only focus on it for seconds at a time. I learned there's nothing wrong with that; it's simply a case of returning to the task. Sometimes the sound of my breath was as good an anchor of focus as anything else. My pulse was returning to normal … it was. In through the nose, out through the mouth. In through the nose, out through the mouth.

Moments after this, I noticed one guy browsing at a book stand about 30 feet from me, with his hand luggage at his side and wearing a blue t-shirt. He looked about late 30s, slim physique with a slight paunch, fair hair that was thinning; he was sipping his coffee minding his own. His t shirt was what caught my eye. It had #BA in big, bold, white font on the front. I felt my teeth grind inside a tense closed mouth. A few moments later, a young woman walked by with her hand luggage … she had a red t-shirt that had #BA in big, bold, white font on the front. I had to shake my nervousness figured I was being grandiose. Shortly after this, a middle-aged guy waddled by with a slight wheeze to his gait, hand luggage in tow with a red baseball cap with a white #SLSG logo on the front. I knew that we'd be boarding in a matter of minutes; I had to put this to the back of my mind. However, when I got on the plane, I saw four more red and blue #BA t-shirts throughout the cabin. I even spotted a #SLSG vinyl sticker on someone's hand luggage. Come to think of it, I could have sworn I saw a bumper sticker or two in the parking lot. Taking my seat and belting up on my way to see an Irupblecan governor in the Bluegrass State, I had only one thought in my mind: "What the fuck is going on?"

DENOUEMENT (PART I)*: French for "when it all goes to hell because these assholes are incapable of learning."*

I entered the commanding office in Frankfort, Kentucky. It was ornate and maintained with a remarkably high ceiling, an old-school conservative style. Thick, polished, gleaming pine made up every angle of the upholstery. I said I entered the office, the thing was the length of a subway platform. The actual desk of this monster office was half a fucking mile away. I thought: "Jesus Christ, they don't even give the President this much office." At the very far end of this corridor of leather-bound books in fine shelves and framed photos of smiling handshakes, there was a small figure behind a large desk.

A short, house elf of a man stepped out. His waist highs hit his nipples and he had slicked back white hair. He looked like if he wasn't in conservative politics he'd be digging for oil, in about 1859. A staggering limp began approaching me from the other end of the room. I could hear his exhales of effort from his breathing. He looked cartoon to me, but he was an elected governor. The phone on his desk started ringing. He stopped his half-mile march towards me, looked back at his desk, turned back towards me, waved his arms like he was directing air traffic and yelled: "FUCK IT, I'M GOING BACK!"

And so he did. He began his waddle back towards his desk at a slightly faster pace. When he eventually reached the desk, he leaned over and grabbed the ringing land line.

"Kelly, what the fuck is it? Ahm. Ahm. You put 'em through then. Hello sir. Yes you are. You are speaking to Governor Darn Tootin, yes sir. Ahm. Ahm. Can I ask some quick questions? Why thank you, sir.

"Do I get to pork barrel?

"Do I get to gerrymander?

"Do I get on C-Span?

"Do I get campaign funding?

"THEN *WHAT THE FUCK ARE YOU CALLING FOR?!?!?*"

The phone was thrown at such velocity that Russell Crowe gulped from another hemisphere. More alarmingly, this miniature old boy, waist highs to the neck, made a sudden 180 to face me.

"Sunshine, I can only say I remember your Father, the work he put in, and I am not surprised—"

As if the colossal, Death Star dimensions of this office were entirely lost on this miniature man, he decided to travel the length of the office to get to me before finishing his remark. Honest to god, this sentence hung in the air for a full three minutes. Before concluding it, he'd finally hobbled right in close to me. Though his shoulders were about waist height, he gripped me with a stupid male caricature of a handshake. You know, the ones that physically hurt yet somehow express nothing.

"That the son is a prodigal one. God bless you sir, god bless you. Everything you said on that Twitter account has been worth it."

The Twitter account. That goddamn Twitter account … my mouth, my stupid fat goddamn mouth that only gets me into trouble. Who had I attracted to this and what had I done? The Governor turned and waddled his way to the nearest, buffed-to-perfection pine surface. He poured two glasses of whiskey from a decanter. He turned back and handed me one with a warm smile.

"Son—"

"Governor. I'm sorry but I've gotta let you down here."

"There's a few words I don't enjoy hearing …"

He wasn't lying. An undercurrent of rage emanated from him in pure heat. Beads of sweat dripped from my forehead instantly; it was like standing next to a volcano. I stammered on the spot, realizing the gravity of what the last few days had taught me: I now … had to explain … that I'd been publicly encouraging people … to shoot themselves. What fun.

"Have a seat son, you're making me nervous," he said, in the grand corridor of finest wood and inch-perfect photo frames. Bizarrely, inside this lengthy, epic of an office was another pointless corridor stretching through its center … made up of couches. This was no social arena for anyone with hope of a life, but nevertheless, endless couches could be found, everywhere. We both lowered ourselves onto one and I began searching for words.

"Governor, we can't possibly go ahead with Save Lives, Save Guns. It's absolutely terrible. I don't even know where to begin with this. It's genuinely awful."

"I hope that's not cold feet I'm hearing ..."

"Yeah, yeah, it is. They are cold, sir. Outright cold. Very cold. Freezing. Dude at the end of *Titanic* levels of coldness. It has to stop, we're gonna end this here."

The minute chap nearly vanished into his waist highs. His freckle-checkered face was aghast for a moment, then somewhat more enraged and menacing. He harrumphed and coughed, took a rich slug of whiskey, and focused on me.

"Look son, I'll hear you out but there's so much for us to discuss and, hey, you got so much momentum, you got so many donations, you—I only hear about this goddamn *#BelieveAmerica* movement. People believe, son. People are ready to *believe* ..."

A harsh chill ran down my spine and the words left me, "Yeah and that means we've got a real cluster on our hands ..."

He looked concerned. "Well, how so?"

I can still remember the trembling terror flowing through my entire body. I could remember weighing up jail time in my head and that was just on the absconded pile of funds this thing had attracted. My throat got tight but I knew I had to talk. I plodded through, searching for words.

"Governor. The initial idea behind this is toxic. Genuinely ... excuse my language, but ... fucked."

He leaned back into the couch, and took a sip of whiskey. "Get to it son, if this thing is a waste of my time, I'd rather know sooner than later."

I zoned out, my mind wandered in self-reflection and a total lack of comprehension. What the hell had my life become? My face didn't move as I spoke.

"Governor. The idea of Saving Lives and Saving Guns, is that ... people shoot themselves ... not lethally, not to die or take their own lives but … yeah … that's my big idea. That's the … Grand Fromage … the high concept … rather than people shooting each other and dying … people shoot themselves and live."

There was silence initially. I took an inhale of breath that heaved my chest so hard my head rolled back. I'd announced to an elected representative that I'd been broadcasting policy that encouraged mass self-harm. Jail time was an ominous bastard of a thought that would not leave. Observing Governor Tootin he swilled the last dregs of whiskey in the tumbler then looked up at me.

"See … that's where you gotta get the homeless involved."

"What???"

"We can seriously reduce deficit and spending if we roll out these measures. Everybody wants to know how much money we're spending on the public. This'll be a great answer to quell those fears."

Half my mouth was hung up in a rye smile. I waited. I looked right at the Governor. My impulse was to speak, but I simply couldn't. So I stared at him and he stared at me. I kept waiting. I was waiting for him to say "gotcha," burst into a laugh. This did not happen.

"You … you cannot be serious."

"Oh, I'm serious. Why I've got over 30 Irupblecan representatives waiting to meet you."

"What?!?"

"You found a way, kid. You are the one. You found a way of saving lives and saving guns."

"But Christ, look at what's gonna happen! People will be shooting themselves thanks to this thing!"

"Oh boyo, hush your little mouth. This is American politics—nobody cares about results. We care about finding the slogan people want to hear, you idiot! You've found that. Now hush up and be happy. Playing with toys you don't understand. People think politics can give them what they want, but the way I see it is, we give the public what we want. We do all the leg work; compromise, right?"

"I don't think you understand the basic premise of democratic representation."

"I don't think you've been to dinner with the lobbying industry the way I have, son, let me tell you—"

"Oh I know the lobbyists, I got hold of one myself—the man is a lunatic. Why listen to those assholes over your own constituents?"

"MONEY, MONEY, MONEY—*MONEH!*"

I was once again in a blur, a flurry of feeling, I didn't know if I was angry or scared or sad, but my voice arrived, it was urgent.

"You want money, huh? Money? Darn, Mr. Tootin, look into my eyes. I will give you every last cent of this PAC, if you don't go ahead with this festering shit of an idea."

"I don't want your money, boy. Not really. I just want power, there ain't nothin' like it. Everyone answers to ya and waits for your turn to speak. People can't do without ya once you get enough of the stuff. You see, I like that. It's like my existence matters and I ain't ever really felt that any other way. People talk about their kids being born but I just got isolated for 20 months by an overweight wife. I prefer politics. I get more out of that than I could out of any pot of gold."

"God oh mighty—but what do you *do* with it? You're supposed to be following through on the wishes of others, that's the whole point. You're an elected representative, you have to govern."

"Or … we don't do anything … let it all fall apart … then blame somebody else for the decay … or just deny the decay all together."

"You're a sociopath."

"*DON'T THROW YOUR SOCIAL SCIENCES AT ME!!!*"

"*OH! To hell with*—What are you even talking about social sciences for?!? Don't ya get what I've just been telling you?! People will get *hurt*. This is a dumb idea, a real dumb idea, I should never have run. People are likely to get hurt by this. This is bad news, Governor! Wake up! Hey, it's real bad shit on your end. This is gonna be disproportionate on anyone who isn't white or a guy."

"Boyo, ain't you cute. I'm a 21st Century Irupblecan officeholder. Haven't you heard? Anyone who isn't white and a guy *is just a hoax invented by the Chinese!*"

It was going to be a full afternoon …

I wondered what Andi would have made of it: admitting scars does little for people without the heart to look at them.

DENOUEMENT: PART II

I had already got up and was pacing. Governor Tootin sat there eyeing me up. Imagine a velociraptor with a southern drawl, in waist highs up to its front claws. I looked out towards his desk at the farthest point of this never-ending room. This was an office of an elected representative; he had to answer to the public. I turned; the southern Dobby had waddled his way back over to the decanter to pour another. I called across to him,

"Darn, if this is such a good idea, why not outright tell the public?" I asked. His shoulders jumped up a little, and he glanced back at me with a smirk.

"Well, did we tell the public about COINTELPRO at the time? No. Did we tell them about the specific details of NAFTA on the American worker? No. Hell, sunshine, we got a pantheon of arms deals and military deployments, lists of stuff the public aren't guided towards. That's how countries work. Grow up, you're beginning to sound like a millennial, for Christ sakes. The public feels lots and thinks little. That's the masses, that's your group psychology comin' in there. The more numbers in the room, the IQ points drop off one by one by one. Now America in totality has over 320 million people living in it. That is ample opportunity to create legions of misguided fucks. Just avoid specifics. Tell 'em what they wanna hear."

"Oh Christ, if you have such antipathy for the public, why work for them?"

"Every constituent I have has wished me dead publicly over eight times, son, yet they never vote me out. I don't get it. I'm gonna have to inhale bath salts out of a hooker's asshole at this rate," the Governor grumbled, looking longingly out the office window.

"Hey! You want the public to go out and shoot themselves?

That's what this means, right? That's what I'm telling you. That's what you're standing for." I wasn't blinking, staring right through the guy.

The round, plodding, whiskey-holding loon slowly waded towards me. His sun-freckled leathery skin showing the age of a good seven decades; he held an expression of easy calm. He sidled up to me and tried to put his arm round my shoulder, but again it was more of a waist hug due to height.

"Sam, right? Samson, I believe," he said, full metal Mephistopheles.

"I don't know how you think you have a justification for people shooting themselves. You must be genuinely deranged."

He chuckled. Clinked his full second tumbler with mine and in a pirouette, the weird Dobby-esque nightmare of a man announced to me: "Liberty."

"OH FOR CRYING OUT LOUD." I bellowed so hard the nearest lamp flickered.

"Freedom."

"Governor, no. No, no, no, no. This is mad. This doesn't—"

"Prosperity."

A torrent of rage shot through me and the explosion of shattering glass filled the corridor. The empty tumbler in my hand had been launched through the glass cabinet behind the Governor. Mr Tootin slowly turned to observe the damage behind him. Darn Tootin slowly scanned over the destruction of his property then turned back to me. I cut in before he had a word.

"Liberty, freedom and prosperity are adjectives and *only fucking adjectives* if they open the doors for mass violence. Call off the troops. Call up the FDA, I don't care. I'm don't give a shit anymore. Send me to jail. I've destroyed the property of a government official. You don't wanna be an accomplice to a felon, do you? Mr. Elected Representative." I had him. I knew I had him. I'd made it. Game over. The Governor hung his head and after a beat, scowled at me.

"Alright, sit down, ya whining sumbitch. Get ya a glass of water. I'll get on the phone, can you please stop breaking my shit," he defeatedly murmured as he made his way back over to the desk. Encouragingly, the Governor first and foremost got me a paper cup of water from the cooler by the whiskey decanter. His face was tight with frustration, but he made his way back over to me.

"I am severely fuckin' disappointed," he said, shaking his head with the cup of water held out for me. "Calm down son, politics is politics. I thought you had something and I was ready to follow it. If you're telling me it isn't going ahead, I guess I don't have a choice, it's your baby. Your right. I'll call off the troops." He sighed; beginning to walk back towards his desk, he called out to me: "You ought to be paying for my fuckin' phone bill for this, by the way."

I accepted the paper cup and sipped the water before slugging it down. Looking round the frames in the room, all the famous faces and famous officeholders. This terrible idea got so close to reality, my whole body began to feel heavy from the relief and the adrenaline drop. Or so I thought. I carefully lowered my body on to the nearest couch, then realized my stomach was in a mild ache and I felt dizzy. I looked over to Governor Darn Tootin; the raptor was back, he had a fixed fierce stare suggesting I was his dinner.

"Whath fu—" My speech was slurred and labored. I could only hear him spilling out a little chuckle as my vision began to blur.

"Whatha fudge avyou done tumme?" was the best edition of talking I could muster. The raptor had crept over and stood before me, kind of. I mean with me sitting down, we were kind of head to head. He had his arms folded and eyes locked in a pensive leer.

"Boyo, I had a bad feeling it would resort to this, but today couldn't be spoiled. It doesn't appear you've grasped what the hell you've started here. Or for that matter, how many people or much capital you've attracted. This is the biggest day of the year. You musta guessed?"

At this point I was half scared I was dying. Between a mangled back, sleep deprivation and now being drugged, I was in agony and utterly defenseless. As for the Governor, I didn't know what the hell the guy was talking about. I just prayed it wasn't the "big day" the Okies were locked and loaded about. The tiny little Governor revved himself up like a 16-year-old in their first car.

"*Good morning Samson Johnson*! Today is the day! Today is the Conservative Political Action Conference and you, sunshine, are our *keynote speaker!*"

Oh shit. Then my eyelids were like lead; all they did was flutter, and I couldn't move my body. That's pretty much the last memory I have of being in the Governor's megalodon office.

DENOUEMENT: PART III

I came to consciousness in a rec room, backstage area of some arena somewhere. All my eyes informed me of were concrete pillars, walls and floors. My eyes then met the worst possible vision to be surrounded by, Darn Tootin and Adam. A pair of oddball, borderline extraterrestrials staring down at me. I heard Adam mumble: "He's back, do you think you gave him enough?"

Darn Tootin growled in response: "Who gives a fuck, we're nearly at the finish line with this thing."

Panic filled me from my ears to my boots, and my legs attempted to jolt me into standing. I was strangely energized. Adam and Darn instantly leaned in to spot me.

"Wow, wow, wow. Steady. Steady."

Inside me was no compulsion to speak. Like a child lost in a Walmart, I kinda waddled about and looked around this backstage lot. There was a cacophony of voices chatting; whatever arena this was, it was filling up. My last memory struck me, I turned to Darn.

"You drugged me," I mumbled in the tone of a confused child.

Darn took a couple of gentle steps forward. "I'm sorry, boyo, you have to understand, this is an almighty important moment—"

A full, deep, ominous rumble started all around us. I could feel it in the floor. I feared the bastards had brought me West the day a fault line opened up. The rumble eased in intensity and remained as an ominous bass-like hum. Ahead of me were double red doors just outside the rec room. I looked to Darn and Adam who were just standing, staring at me. Shoulder first I barged the left of the red doors and light from the outside spilled in. Lines of coaches filled my eyesight as I took in the parking lot. There was an entire fleet of coaches, the last of which was finally pulling up. One by one, their automatic doors slid and lowered open like a domino effect. Then they appeared. First I saw shoes; well, it was mainly sandals and socks. Then the parking lot slowly filled with middle-aged people in various shades of beige and grey. Then the dog collars became visible. Then the bibles could be seen in every other hand. The Evangelicals, the most powerful political demographic in the country. How the hell had Adam and Darn got hold of them?

Adam's hand squeezed my shoulder. "Sam. This is the yard line. Getting you on that stage and delivering the speech for the #BelieveAmerica movement is the goal. The moment you are saying the words you need to, the game's won. Superbowl. NBA Finals. World Cup. Olympics. This is the field goal, Sam, we just need you to kick."

I remember running my hand across my brow. "To continue the analogy Adam, sure it's a field goal but unfortunately, some deranged idiot has filled the ball with Semtex."

Adam frowned and pushed further. "Think of the guns, Sam, think of the good this could do."

"Jesus, not you too. What good? We're laying down a plan that gets people to fire guns at themselves."

Adam grimaced with discomfort. He then nodded. He then looked up at me. "See, this is where I think the Governor's suggestion of involving the homeless—"

"OH FUCK ME." I bellowed so hard some cement crumbled from a nearby pillar.

Two hands, wiry and wrought with tension, grabbed the bottom of my lapels. Darn Tootin's fury scratched voice fired at me. "Listen, you stupid sum'bitch. You can't be getting moral and indignant when you started the very fucking thing you're complaining about. How many people did you lie to? How much bullshit did you spread? How much disinformation have you been peddling … comrade?"

"Hey, hey, hey, I didn't lie to anybody. No wait, that is objectively not true. But I didn't set out to mislead people, I—"

"Left out the specifics? Like I've been advising since the moment we met. Kid, *give the fuck up*. You had an idea, you thought you'd do good, you haven't. Now your idea is being bought out by people with more capital than you, deal with it. This is America, profit is king. You could be a fucking hero if you let the right people open up revenue streams out of this."

"But people are dying and that needs to stop, Governor. Maybe we can check our wallets after everyone's taken goddamn care of?!?"

"So now you don't wanna save the guns, you got no respect for the Constitution?"

A lump in my throat arrived with such a harsh sharpness it could have sunk a cruise liner. My voice wobbled like shit and I gave him the last ounces I had in the tank.

"This isn't about guns, Governor. Listen to me! This is about me and I'm the problem. I'm lacking, I'm weak, I'm stupid, I'm a boy in man's clothes; I look out and see what's wrong with the world and I wanna change it. With my whole shriveled, pointless heart I do, but I can't. I want all the bad and all the people doing bad to stop in their tracks and I can't make that happen. I know I wake up in the morning and bad things are going to go down and I am powerless to stop that. I can commit, I can work, I can apply myself in every direction of need I really want but terrible things are gonna happen no matter how much I do. No matter how much anyone does. That is a pain I need to learn to live with.

"I've cooked up a mad plan, spread it across the country, whipping up a fever like I've found a miracle, when there is no miracle. There is no one person who can solve these ills. This movement is reckless shit that does not help anybody. Solutions that work can't come easy, they need earning. Through listening to people, through communicating ideas, through sharing perspectives, it can't all be me, me, me, me. This PAC, this idea, it's no good. We need to deal in reality. We need to hang up the myths and dreams for just one moment. We can get back to them when basic safety isn't a roulette for the young, but we've got an almighty problem here and we need to move on this thing. Do you understand? Are you listening to me, goddamn it! Everything is not alright, it isn't; we need to be adult enough to take that now."

Tootin's harsh frown was angled down towards the floor.

"Why ... that was very interesting, boyo. I am awfully glad you've been on a journey of inner whatever. Now, I've got a whipped-up crowd expecting a miracle, so could you shut the fuck up and excuse me a moment."

The Governor barged through with his elbows. Due to stature, that meant a timely strike in the crotch for me. I then nearly killed myself as I was standing on his red tie. The thing was the length of a ticker tape roll. With Darn Tootin's height the thing looked more like a dog lead. Anyway, the crusty old geezer yanked the tie from under me and as I nearly completed a backflip, his last words were a passionate snarl.

"Would you FUCK OFF."

He made his way through a dark blue curtain and took to the stage beyond after his name was announced and met with enthusiastic applause. With assistance of a small step ladder, Governor Tootin occupied the podium. He thanked the crowd and began addressing why he was there. It was for the SLSG PAC. The nightmare kept unfolding, and I was powerless to stop it. My eyes glazed over, looking on at the wooden floor of the stage. Watching the Governor's mouth, it seemed to be in slower than slow motion. My heart dropped a foot as eager faces on the front few rows met my line of vision. The cat was out of the bag. A husky nasal sound hovered by my right shoulder. Lungs that suggested the condition of decades old vacuum bags; it could only be Adam.

"He's the warm-up guy. All in. You better be ready."

"Adam, when did I agree to be keynote speaker at the Conservative Political Action Conference?"

"Unconsciously ... with a pen ... that your hand was wrapped around ... that my hand was wrapped around ... while you were asleep."

Searching for words in my shellshock, I couldn't make a sound. Adam's smoking-torched throat continued its roll.

"Hey. You weren't around for a few months. You missed some highlights. This is only recently, take a look."

Adam pulled a slender tablet from a jacket pocket and sidled next to me so the screen was visible to us both. He pulled up the YouTube app and began playing a clip. A weird pull tugged at the bottom of my chest the moment I saw the title of the video:

Academy Awards: Best Actor Acceptance Speech

An actress in a dress three times the price of her life's earnings gave a 12-minute soliloquy complimenting men she probably knew belonged on offenders registers. Then, low and behold, Tim Della Haklin took to the stage. In his defense, he looked pretty fresh in a tux, but I still felt incredibly unnerved being shown this by Adam. A plume of musky cigar smoke floated by and Adam's voice purred: "He did it, our boy, The Bushman, you gotta see this."

Looking into the screen, Adam turned up the volume and I soon witnessed the Tim Della Haklin Oscar speech.

"I just wanna say, this is all about me. I'm gonna mention some names now that nobody's heard of in order to avoid a soft blacklisting and preserve my career for the next 20 minutes. Like most award winners, I'm in for some real shitty scripts after this. The films are gonna get progressively worse as I get older, more commodified, less appreciated and increasingly lose the integrity in my work. To think, all it took was a bowling trophy and room full of clapping seals to give me a sense of validation and now I'm here. I'm not entirely sure why I spent the best part of 25 years chasing this...ah well, with my kind of money, you can have as many addictions and recoveries as a lifetime can fit in. But as the orchestra now comes in and cuts off

this cascade of self-seeking garbage, I feel a need to advertise to the public that I'm a wonderful human being.

"The guys over at the #BelieveAmerica movement in recent months are bringing home the gravity of gun violence in this country. I'm all for those guys and the ambition of what they are after. You know what, in a time of total division, let's respect all, let's Save Lives and Save Guns; then everybody's being heard in America and everybody gets to be a part of making it a better place. God bless this country, god bless the Academy, and good night."

It was like watching ISIS behead Mister Rogers. A ferocious panic attack followed and Adam offered me his cigar for help. I nearly punched his lights out. In fairness to the demented prick, he then got me a chair and stabilized me back to normal respiratory function. The cat had been out of the bag all the time I was away. I was looking at the makings of a lifetime in prison. Strange enough, my utter lack of soul invigorated Adam's.

"So you're a hunchback now? That is fantastic. You could raise all kinds of funds for people with these kinda things."

"Ah, shut up, Adam. This is a selfish debauched wreck and I'm accountable. I'm gonna bomb that goddamn speech. I'm left with no choice. This is stupid and dangerous. This is telling people to shoot themselves!!"

"What are you talking like that for? Hey. Are you feeling OK? Any … warmth? Any kinda … desire to move? You know, dance?"

Watching Adam attempt to dance was the only genuine moment of levity in about ten years for me. He wobbled like a palm tree in a gale with the physique of the Goodyear tire man. It was a revelation. Through a long-needed smile, I continued my resignation, albeit in a softer tone.

"Game over, Adam. I'll meet ya back down on planet earth anytime. We're in big trouble here and that might be what we deserve."

Adam hissed away my "waffle" and got out a fold of paper from his jacket breast pocket. His fluffy, podgy finger poked at the stats he pulled out in front of me. I was kind of agitated and barked, "What is this? Polling?"

"Polling?? Gimme a break, I've always asked rich people around bars in DC. Why do you think most of the public have been miserable for 40 years? We keep telling them they're telling us what they aren't telling us: it all makes sense."

"How have I hired literally the worst DC has to offer?? What are the fucking odds? I'm more likely to have been anointed the Pope. You guys are such assholes. The depth of your assholery is— you're not even assholes anymore; you're rectums. You're the entire cavity. I ju—"

I felt all flushed a second, then an inhale of breath struck me like a harsh wind. Something drove me breathless. Then my whole body started to feel warm. A cozy, fluffy tingle started to coat my body. My mood began to rise and I just felt ... great.

"What's ... going on?" I inquired with a royal grin on my face. Adam's face was glowing with the most disarming gentle smile I had ever seen. Adam was beautiful. Then I heard his voice which was again, gorgeous, "So it's finally kicking in. Great! Right on time," Adam said, as the lobbyist increasingly became angelic according to my senses. He offered a high five and it looked like the most original idea of all time.

"What's kicking in?" I chimed breezily, giving him five.

"A little champion's wake up."

"You're so poetic, man. I know I've been mean to you, but you are so beautiful, Adam. I mean that, man. You're, like, one of the most capable and breathtaking human persons ... I've ever encountered."

These words poured out of me. I was about to find out why.

"That's the MDMA talking, but you've also been given a little Charlie, lil Adderall, some pure Guarana flakes, goji powder and about four weeks' worth of caffeine tablets."

I looked down at my feet to make sure I was still on the ground and I was ... I just couldn't feel my feet. My vision appeared to have refracted entirely as certain areas of the backstage now shined purple and orange in thin glowing lines intermittently. I will live with regret for a long time and I've been able to reflect, substance use is something I should leave to other people, but my next words were:

"You guys are goddamn legends! If you had pussies I'd mattress dance the shit out of ya. We're gonna make history here. Get me on that stage. LETS DO THIS! TIM DELLA HAKLIN BAY-BAY! OH YEEEEEEAAAHHHH!!!!!!"

DENOEUMENT: THE FINALE

It was the CPAC, it was my crowd, hell, it was my "base." I had an idea that could end deaths by the bullet forever without taking guns away. Approaching the stage from the back, I had a firm suspicion I could walk out of here with Breitbart declaring, "JESUS FOUND, MARYLAND!" My heart was pounding about 200 beats a second; if I wasn't big boned, I probably would have taken flight. I heard the angry, short, little guy before me say my name, well, try to: "Satsum Jogsoon." I guess I'll be him today.

Making it onto the stage felt like my legs were moving faster than the speed reality was running at. I was scared I was going to park me badly and crash into the podium. Then, I found myself at the podium in front of an applauding crowd and I even got a couple of wolf whistles. The adulation died down quickly though, and I had to get on with talking. Quiet was ushered into a silence. Finally, it was just me on my own with my chance to spread the message. I took a breath so deep it hit my asshole, and, high as a kite, I figured, to hell with it, I'm doing this.

"Good evening, it is a pleasure to be among people who love this country and among fellow Americans. I want to thank you all for turning out, it means a lot to me and the more I've been thinking these days, I know the more we turn out for each other, the more we're willing to listen and to work for each other, then the more love we have in God's eyes, so thank you for that."

THUNDEROUS APPLAUSE. Always good to get in the "God stuff," clearly a winner with this crowd.

"I don't need to tell a room full of sharp-minded patriots like yourselves that on any given social or political issue right now our country is in fragments. We, we finally got our political conscience engaged on a large scale as a nation and that means we now can't agree on a single thing."

Less applause this time but a lot of nodding heads and a few of the gals elbowing the gals next to them.

"What I've always wanted for our country was to find the right path with guns because let's face it my friends, there are far too many Americans dying today by the bullet and this is not the vision our founders held when writing our Constitution. When the Founders wrote the Second Amendment they held a vision of America where every homestead should be safe, and no man's wealth or livelihood held back my another's malice, but look where we find ourselves. Our schools, places of worship, places of social freedom are getting shot at. I ask you, is this not the kind of tyranny our Founders wished to save us from? So where do we go? What can our choices be? We the people of these United States find our Constitution at an impasse with morality, so where do we go, I ask you?"

Feedback from the crowd began.

"GOD!"

"TALK TO JESUS. BEST DAMN AMERICAN EVER BORN IN BETHLEHEM!"

"READ THE WORDS OF THE LORD."

"Amen to that my friends, for that is exactly where we must turn because it is in 'GOD WE TRUST'!"

I was getting endless whistles and a real pop from the crowd now; it was something special. I felt like a band that had come back on for the encore.

"We cannot betray our line to exceptionalism and that is what the founders handed us in the form of our Constitution and this is the very essence God looks for in every one of us. So, when we hear our friends on the left say we should hand in all our guns, we are truly betraying God."

"Nobody here wanna betray him," a voice yelled out from a sea of boos.

"I know he doesn't want us to, but he knows we are betraying him every time we have another one of our schools, our colleges drown in a spray of gunfire. So, we must look to Romans—"

I had Googled "Bible quotes on sacrifice"; it's amazing what the internet can do for you now.

"Therefore, I urge you, brothers and sisters, in view of God's mercy, to offer your bodies as a living sacrifice, holy and pleasing to God—this is your true and proper worship."

The room was in my palm, the whole place was waiting in anticipation.

"We cannot continue in escalation and retaliation, but in repentance and in sacrifice, this is our only way forward in gun violence. We cannot return bullets with bullets. We must turn the bullets on ourselves."

A lot less applause now and a whole lotta confused faces, but a handful of absolute enthusiasts in the middle loved it. I took a brief pause to take in the place. Rapture is what they call a moment; when attention is given in such scale, all else disappears—I had that, and it was electric, then my mouth ran away again.

"Our bodies ... a living sacrifice ... this is possible, but you must *believe* America! If you're tired of cops fearing Black folks and Black folks fearing cops, then you must believe America. If you're tired of everyone getting poorer and poorer while the rich still profit, then you must believe America. If you're wanting a healthcare system that doesn't ever fail you and leave millions to die, then you must believe America. If you want to see a day when the wages in the shining city on a hill match the cost of living here, then you must believe America! If you're tired of the Constitution being used as a pawn for other people's arguments and only that, then YOU MUST BELIEVE AMERICA! For what is the Second Amendment but an opportunity to pop a cap in an ass? Well, there's an old saying that "each one, teach—"

BANG.

I hit the floor instantly and there was a lot of screaming. I'll be honest, I hadn't planned to sign off the speech by shooting myself. I should have probably run that by HR first, but hey. Turns out even a buttock wound is incredibly painful. My therapist says my ability to process excitement is one of my "big projects."

Oh, and the gun? I got that off some guy. He only asked me for a driver's license, yeah, that was it. Just a guy, living in a van … *down by the river*.

Epilogue

WELL, YOU'RE NOT GONNA BELIEVE this ... but I resurrected on the third day. Not much of a resurrection in truth. Just got out of a rare coma induced by a double drugging and shooting myself in the ass. What followed was a prolonged period of being detained by the authorities. First, the Maryland authorities, which was mainly being stuck in grey and pastel-colored interrogation rooms. I was informed that someone at the Southern Poverty Law Center had flagged my visit as "alarming." I was soon transferred over to New York district court. This was a lot scarier as this was when the FBI stepped in. There were several hundred hours spent in litigation, interrogation and dealing with legal counsel. The woman they hired as legal counsel for me was superb; there was not a single bead of sweat dropped at any single moment. However, two weeks in, she left her post on clear grounds: "I now need to find my own legal counsel thanks to going near your mess."

The next legal counsel was male and sweating all over the fucking shop. He said he'd been sober for 15 years before taking my case, but that changed in the first six hours. Michael was typically in a grey blazer and, at the beginning of proceedings, usually halfway through a sub. He was sharp on litigative detail, but not so much on me.

"Just plead insanity, I'm guessing that's what happened here. Who on earth knows ..."

I soon found myself sitting in a hearing room of one of the New York district courtrooms. Man, never go to court, I tell you; those places make a person feel incredibly small and I guess that's the point. The reports of public reaction to the CPAC and the #BelieveAmerica movement were consequential enough in themselves. I was informed that 18 copycat chapters of the "movement" had been started nationwide. This meant sad groups of left-leaning libertarians, mad enough to believe shooting themselves with a gun could actually make a difference. However, they really did believe and really did shoot themselves (thigh, shoulder, calf, buttock), and I had explaining to do: to most of America. This thing got popular. I was too busy flying round like an overmedicated, Quasimodo rip-off to see that SLSG PAC was getting attention from TV's many talking heads. Most moderate candidates were name dropping it on campaign stops. You see, this—the campaigns, the politicians, the media getting all pissy and shitty—I couldn't really care about. But the people … oh man, I'll never say sorry enough till I'm dead.

I was looking up at a TV screen in an interrogation room waiting for police officers to organize the next round of escorting me. It was beautiful … the sight that my eyes laid upon was more than I could ever have imagined. People got in on this, people got it. T-shirts followed the shares, the retweets, the likes and all that social media bullshit. There was Irupblecan red with a giant white #BA on the front and a tweet across the back. There was Cremodat blue with a giant white #BA on the front and a tweet across the back. Sure it was a stupid news thing, sure it wasn't the entire country, but the reds and the blues *were talking*. The different sides made an effort to meet in the middle. My heart swelled and dropped the moment I saw the report showing the grills, fish fries, beers and coffees shared. These guys were willing to go. There was a swath of quite remarkable people capable of making change happen. There was a many million strong army who could go to war against children being laid to waste, of continual pointless slaughter, of a track record none of us are proud of. My gaze hit the floor; I wasn't a part of this awe-inspiring legion. I was part of the small cohort of toxic, self-adoring jagoffs leading them to their lessening. I'd failed them badly. In my addled state, I'd managed to pay tribute to and over-look the number one cause of gun death in America—suicide. Yeah … people weren't happy with me and rightfully so.

I was sentenced to life in a sanitorium. This on the grounds that I was clearly an individual of little contact with reality, yet mirac-ulously capable at the same time. I needed "1-1 observation levels" to say the least. The insanity plea worked and, frankly, worked on two grounds:

1) The judge could not make one iota of sense out of what the hell I'd actually done here. That guy asked for a repeat of so many statements out of genuine bewilderment, from everyone who talked. Darn Tootin's performative testimony was his only reprieve. The judge looked pissed and upset from the opening statements. Come the end, he didn't look any better …

2) Most pertinently in my case, as an individual standing trial in this country, pasty pale white boys aren't the priority of America's criminal justice system. This isn't right, and I'm not proud.

The judge took one last look at me before adjourning the jury to reach a verdict, and it was a seminal moment. He asked me in an clear inquiring tone: "Why did you do all this, son?"

The courtroom's gallery of faces filled my eyes. My chest heaved and my throat wrenched tight. I was physically shaking, and on hot breath it spilled out of me,

"I just couldn't take any more children dying."

So began a four-hour sobbing fit as I was escorted from the stand uncontrollably shaking. Michael later told me my "collapse" had "saved" me. I didn't feel saved, and I meant every syllable. More to the point: children are still regularly dying under the gun in

America, and in truth, if trend lines are left unopposed, the rest of us aren't all that safe either.

I know I said I didn't mind how the media behaved, but a word to the wise: don't leave yourself open for the goddamn media. They reported me like I was the world's worst Travis Bickle. I was like Travis Bickle and Biff Loman sired the world's most disappointing bastard. This between being denounced as a malicious, diamond-eyed ideologue. There was a list of PR hungry, status obsessed, Gen X goons out to dog pile me because they hadn't made anything memorable in over a decade. A few came out and gave tear stick magazine interviews about how "used" they felt by Samson Johnson's *#BelieveAmerica.* They only made 5k a paragraph, yet how magically verbose they became …

In fairness to the satire guys, they nailed me; it was a scorched earth policy, rolling thunder for six long months. Of course, *The Daily Show* summed it up with gravity:

"So after all this lunacy, after all this corrupt batshit madness, people are asking, where is America on guns now? After all the hullabaloo. You know, that's a good question. 'Cus actually, once you strip through the ideas and the madness and the bullshit, you see what's there: isolated, white male, with a headful of bad ideas, a gun in his hand, and we've got a lot of hurt people. This of course takes headlines over the everyday shootings of African Americans and persons of color across Chicago, Detroit, Milwaukee, Cleveland, Delaware, you name it. America's right where it was, baby; hasn't moved an inch on guns."

So for me, it's psych ward life. You know, it's not so bad. The healthcare assistants take me out for a vape on the grounds two or three times a day. On the weekends, usually as a ward, we order some pretty good take away. About four or five weeks ago now, we had our last "incident" with Alana attacking one of the staff. The fewer "incidents" there are on the ward, the more privileges we get; this weekend we were actually allowed to pick a movie totally of our own choosing. We've got a few self-harmers, so no horror, gory movies tend to be a "no-no." As things currently stand, it's no trips out for the foreseeable future. You do get a lot of time in these environments to think. I've not found the thinking aspect so great. I'm pretty blocked emotionally from the meds, but I only harbor regret over all this. Days are long.

I've kind of made it my mission to try and get to know everyone here a little better. Alana said people were fascinated and intimidated when they heard I was coming. Thomas has made the most effort with me, I feel. I meant what I said by the way; the guy *can* draw, his art is really good. Yet, as you can imagine, between the group therapy sessions and being in the same place every day … I don't get up to much. I guess that's the point. Most of my time, I pace the main corridor making up the majority of the ward. There's a little kitchenette up the top and the staff office opposite, but I just walk the main gangway. Sometimes I play music, sometimes I don't know if I feel safe doing so. But yeah, that's me, walking the corridor, up and down, up and down, up and down.

My advice, sitting in a psych ward that looks to be the place I die: if you're feeling bad about life, avoid politics, maybe try therapy. However, if you're feeling bad about the conditions people face in life that can be changed for the better, go talk to people, get every angle of the matter possible, particularly the voices of those you don't immediately think of or those not in your immediate zone of comfort. There's an age-old law that is bigger than any and all of us: If you don't really know how to help, your input might not actually be helpful. We may not get each other, but we will always live with each other. We need to talk. #BelieveAmerica.

About the Author

AFTER SEVERAL YEARS working and writing in London, the author now lives in a quiet corner of Scandinavia, enjoying a balcony view, a fine lady and a fur baby. That is all.